Alibis of the Heart

Darryl Sollerh

Alibis of the Heart
Copyright Darryl Sollerh 2013
Published by Del Oro Company
All Rights Reserved
ISBN: 978-0-9897535-0-0

Alibis of the Heart

Small towns twist and turn on their own logic.

A visitor needs to understand that, especially down in the bayou where the locals have a sixth sense for sussing out who belongs, and who best be on their way.

Because what they won't tell you down in Dixie, as gregarious as they can sometimes seem, is that the best kept secret of 'southern hospitality' has always been to so overwhelm a guest with kindness that you not only feel compelled to speed your own departure, sure that you must be imposing, but, incapable of ever repaying your host's largesse, never to return.

So should you come across a sign bearing a greeting like 'Welcome to Okefenokee', a small town sunk deep into the loam and rot of its namesake swamp, it behooves you to bear in mind the subversive, southern spirit in which it is offered.

And that, as the saying goes, would be Will's first mistake.

But a week before Will would watch his marriage go south, then flee south to lick his wounds, another matter was about to make life even murkier down in the wilds of Okefenokee, rising from its dark places on a moonless night like a specter to throw out the welcome mat for a long-seething rage.

And it went like this…

As a clock crawled past the witching hour in Bubba's Bar, a small, roadside watering hole on the banks of the swamp, a lone black customer in his fifties was hunched over the bar while a young, white bartender with a wife and baby waiting at home hustled to lock up for the night:

Come on, buddy, time ta go.

The black man rallied:

In that case, how about one for the road?

The bartender gave him a look, pointing to the empty shot glass in front of him:

That was your one for the road.

The man shrugged:

So I'm a little drunk. Got my money's worth, right?

All the more reason to go on.

The man grinned:

On and on, all night long!

Toasting his own prowess, he finally slid unsteadily from his stool and teetered out into the dark.

Outside, in the pitch of the swamp's night, the man lurched forward, moving along a small footpath hugging the swamp's sticky banks, smelling of brine, semen and decay.

He then stopped short, not sure if he was headed in the right direction, and then started off again, uncertain, humming an off-key tune.

As he rounded a dark bend under a canopy of hanging Spanish moss, an assailant suddenly emerged from the shadows, tripping and shoving him forward, forcing him face down into the thick mud.

As the disoriented man groped for air, a muddy boot stepped firmly onto the back of his neck, pressing his face inexorably into the ooze. And though the man struggled to free himself, he soon succumbed to suffocation.

It would be a week later, under a heavy morning rain, that Sheriff Reynolds would climb from his cruiser to investigate the just-discovered corpse, marking yet another suspicious demise on the overgrown banks of the swamp.

As Reynolds' thick, grim, white features endured the downpour, his deputy, a black, rail-thin officer Hails, first on the scene, hiked back up to the cruiser, shrugging:

Maybe he drowned accidental, Sheriff.

Reynolds didn't buy that for a moment:

Just like the other one?

As Hale reconsidered, Reynolds inquired:

Ya find his wallet?

Hale shook his head.

And don't nobody recognize him?

He's swolled up pretty bad, Sheriff.

Reynolds looked around, wondering who else may have seen what:

Then I guess its deja-vu all over again.

A bright, clear sky greeted Chicago that morning, lending it a crisp, invigorating energy. It was the kind of day to take a brisk walk through the downtown with its bustle, gleam and its waterways all humming with the steady din of car motors and horns; it was the kind of day to get outside, to feel the cool breezes off the lake, to feel alive.

But not for Will, because despite the magnificent, windswept views from his firm's law offices on the 12th floor, Will's colleague, Jim, was holding an ominous manila envelope in his hands.

Look, the firm's guy did this as a professional courtesy, but it's as your friend now that I'm asking you to just…forget it. Let it go.

Will, handsome, unshaven, his forties eyes red and bloodshot, still wearing the rumpled suit he slept in last night, stared back, unmoved.

So Jim tried again:

You and Brenda've got six good years in your marriage. With some counseling, couple's therapy, who knows, maybe you two could work it out…? But looking at crap like this can only make the healing process that much more…difficult. And for what?

Will shrugged:

For me, Jim. I have to know, Jim. It's just the way I am.

Will then held out his hand, so Jim reluctantly handed over the envelope.

As Will calmly slid out the raw, candid photos, Jim winced like a man watching his pal eat dung.

Will stoically picked through the uncensored photos, appraising the entwined subjects as if they were little more than passing acquaintances.

He takes a good picture. Better than Brenda. But then maybe that's just because of the position she's got herself in there…

Will then held up one of the photos, angling it as if to estimate gravity's axis point:

She always was limber.

Jim looked down, filling with anxiety, wondering perhaps about the intransigencies of his own marriage.

But that's another story.

A week later, Will, now shaven, dressed in jeans and standing in the condo he called home until very recently, dropped the last of his chotchkies into a cardboard box and then traded a testy look with Brenda's smug cat, Buddy.

I'll miss you, too, Buddy.

Will then tried to carry out a favorite armchair. But as he struggled with its unwieldy weight, he succumbed to the moment and broke down, sinking headfirst into its cushion for a brief, private sob.

Pulling himself back together, he scrawled out a note – 'You keep it' – tossed it onto the chair and scooped up his box.

But as he strode for the door, the box's bottom gave way, dumping its entire contents out onto the hardwood floors.

As his mementos scatter-danced away like the pieces of his life, Will stared off for a fleeting moment, feeling cursed.

Gathering himself once more, he summoned a defiant smirk, bowed royally to Buddy, flipped that feline the finger, spun on his heel and marched out, leaving behind a home, a marriage and a career, along with a box full of knickknack memories wherever they lay.

Minutes later, ensconced in his refurbished 1967 Chevy ragtop, Will sped south, his radio belting out R&B tunes along his journey from the northern climes of his youth to the flat, steamy southern expanses, stretching out green, lush and wild as far as the eye could see.

On the way, he endured the requisite brawl with a wind-buffeted road map as landmarks streaked past before he could identify them.

Later, tooling down another stretch of open highway, he tried to chomp into wax-paper-covered burger, only to bite more wax paper than burger, compelling him to un-chomp it back out of his mouth, only to then have to spend the next fifteen minutes retrieving the half-chewed chunks from his crotch to toss out the window.

Last but never least, Will, growing sleepy at the wheel, dozed off, allowing his Chevy to drift across several lanes of highway before being shocked awake and swerving back onto the road.

Finally, mercifully, the endless signs begin to announce he is nearing Okefenokee County, Georgia. And though he still had a long way to travel, he eased, feeling as if he'd taken the next, necessary step in his life, whatever the future, and Okefenokee might hold in store for him – which brings us up date.

So as the last miles seemed to slide off into the humid, overcast afternoon, he exited the highway and coasted onto a connecting road. And after another half an hour's drive, he arrived at a small strip mall with an aging Laundromat, a local diner and a small real estate office…

Will parks and climbs out stiffly to walk to the diner, dropping a dime for a local newspaper on his way in.
But as he tries to enter, he ends up fighting with the diner door's push/pull mechanism, making a brief racket as he enters, drawing the attention of a few locals slow-chewing their late lunches.
Will declines the coffee counter in favor of a row of naugahyde booths, and moves off to them.
Sliding into one, he peruses a tabletop lunch menu. As he looks it over, he notes but ignores the subtle glances still floating his way and looks around for a waitress.
And that's when he sees Jasmine, a southern exotic in a powder-blue uniform she makes look plush, with honey-colored eyes that can take you places in a glance, sunset auburn hair eager to escape her hair pins, and smooth peach skin, glowing with the aura of a woman who's old enough to know.
Her languid, mesmerizing movements instantly draw Will in, compelling yet beguiling his attention.
As he stares at her, trying to understand her sudden grip on his tingling senses, a ratty old man at the coffee counter confronts Jasmine:
Jus' for the record, when I ordered a sandwich, I expect it ta be on white toast. Not rye bread. Whoever heard of tuna on rye?

Jasmine eyes the man flatly and then says:

Don't ever change, honey. I wanna forget ya just the way you are.

She then moves past him, and Will quickly looks away so as not to let her catch him spying. But two beats later he hears:

So what'll it be, honey?

Will looks up to find Jasmine eyeing him with a blunt but wily gaze, as if she can't decide whether to play it straight, or take him for the ride of his life.

Uh, cup of coffee.

Ya gonna order somethin ta eat?

Maybe in a bit.

Jasmine slides her order pad into her womanly hip pocket and moves off, instantly tuning him out.

He watches after her, surprised to find himself beset by a sudden, unexpected case of flirtatus interruptus.

Later, as he combs through the real estate rental ads in the local rag, Jasmine checks her watch impatiently and then moves to Will:

Ya gonna order somethin or not?

Think I'll just stick with the coffee.

Jasmine unceremoniously rips his check from her pad and drops it onto the table. Then she moves off, clearly irked.

Will, sensing it's time to go, gets up and moves to pay the check, forcing Jasmine, now at the end of her shift and covering for the cashier, to ring up his bill – at which Will hears himself say:

I do something wrong?

If ya mean that in the Biblical sense, no, honey. But ya sure could use a little geography lesson when it comes ta eatin establishments like this one.

Enlighten me.

Jasmine eyes him a testy beat as if she might not. But then:

That there's a coffee counter. And just like its name suggests, it's for coffee. Whereas them there are booths, for when you're gonna order something ta eat. I know it don't seem like much to a casual observer, but by the end of a shift, everybody's feet in here knows the difference.

6

Will takes her lesson on the chin:

Sorry. Next time.

As Jasmine ker-chings the register, causing the cash drawer to slide open, she allows:

Next time.

She takes out a penny – his change – and places it in his palm, causing Will to suddenly feel the need to volunteer:

I'm new in town.

She eyes him flatly:

Why, I'm shocked, flummoxed and flabbergasted!

Will takes that on the chin, too.

What I meant was, I was wondering if you might know of a place for rent by the swamp? A small house or cottage maybe?

Nothin comes ta mind, honey.

Well if something does—

But Jasmine's already moving off to 'marry' the ketchup bottles.

So Will takes the hint and heads for the door, only to once again fight with the push/pull mechanism, drawing Jasmine's wry attention:

One side 'pushes', honey, and the other 'pulls'. Just like a romance.

Will, finally managing to open the door, nods back embarrassed as Jasmine, apparently out of mercy, suggests:

Ya might wanna try the realtor next door.

Will looks back:

Pardon?

I said: ya might try the realtor. Right next ta the Laundorama.

The Laundorama?

Ya can't miss it, darlin. He's the only realtor we got.

Will smiles, encouraged by her suggestion:

I'm Will. Will Woods.

Well good for you, honey.

Will takes that too on the chin and, with his tail now firmly between his legs, cuts his losses and leaves.

A few minutes later he finds himself seated in the realtor's office, looking at Dewey McKnight, a short, youthful fifties with his own peculiar way of pronouncing words.

As Will notes a plaque of Appreciation from the National Nature's Conservancy on the wall, Dewey flips through a small box of index cards. So much for computers.

Got your heart set on a place down by the swamp, eh?

Will nods, adding:

My family used to vacation down there. Doesn't have to be anything fancy.

Dewey has to smile:

Fancy? Down by the swamp? Trust me, friend, there's no danger of fancy down by the swamp. Alligators? Yes. But fancy?

Dewey suddenly plucks out one of the cards:

Speakin of which, think I found one for ya...

A short drive later Will finds himself standing with Dewey in a rustic, wooded community sprinkled with white cottages, mostly rundown, but still somehow quaint.

Dewey indicates a big, red For Rent sign hanging in one of the cottage's windows, and Will declares:

I'll take it.

Dewey looks over at him, confused:

Don't ya wanna see inside it first?

If I did, would I take it?

Dewey has to agree:

Probably not.

Exactly. That is why I'll take it.

Late that afternoon, Will wanders down to a small dock to gaze out at the blue-dappled waters, silvery-green grasses and arching trees, hearing the occasional call of a crane accompanying the constant croaking of frogs and buzzing of flies, all riding the humid air of Okefenokee's deep, wild expanse.

With his heart and mind filling with childhood memories, Will sits down to dangle his feet off the edge of the small dock.

He then pulls out his wallet a wedding photo of Brenda.

Taking a last, anguished look, he suddenly tears it up, letting the pieces flutter away on the breeze like tiny white butterflies.

He then takes out a very old, small photo of himself as a young boy, standing in front of a wide stretch of Okefenokee Swamp.

He's holding hands with a fatherly looking man who seems to be in his thirties with a big handkerchief stuffed in his back pocket, but whose face is turned away from the camera.

He eyes the photo and then turns it over to find 'Willy and Dad – Summer' scrawled on the back, triggering not only more memories, but reminding him of a long-kept, stinging secret still haunting his life.

At that very moment, a few miles away in a small county Coroner's office, the Coroner, an odd looking man with squirrel cheeks, was pulling a plastic covered body, still in need of identification, from a freezer.

Sheriff Reynolds, looking on impatiently, asks:
So?
Looks like this one drowned on mud. Sucked it clear right down into his lungs.
Any idea who he is?
The Coroner curls a lip:
Soon as I know, you'll know, Sheriff. Just like always. Now can I do my job?

Back on the docks, as the evening dims into lavender-laced hues, Will walks back up the lane from the dock, only to see a worn-out Buick Rambler gliding up to a neighboring cottage…with none other than Jasmine at the wheel.

He watches, part incredulous, part pleased, and part annoyed as she climbs from the Rambler and goes into her cottage home, adjacent to his cottage.

Will then looks over at the large, unavoidable For Rent sign still hanging in his new window and smirks – she couldn't miss it even if she tried.

He then looks back over at her cottage as its lights come on, glowing up warmly and innocently behind her cotton curtains, causing Will to shake his head, and head on in for the night.

Early the next morning, Will strides into the diner and angles for the coffee counter, ignoring another round of suspicious looks from the regulars.

He takes a seat and waits patiently for Jasmine to finally come over:

Remember me?

Like it was yesterday.

It was yesterday.

Like I said.

Will presses on:

Then no doubt you also remember I was looking for a place to rent?

Lord knows we're all lookin for somethin, honey.

And speaking of looking, did you happen to notice anything unusual about the cottage right across from yours?

If ya mean that big, red, obnoxious For Rent sign hangin in the window, how could ya miss it?

You can't.

Have ta be deaf, dumb and blind to miss an eyesore like that.

Exactly.

Will waits for Jasmine to crumble under his blistering cross-examination, only she isn't crumbling.

Instead, she seems to be waiting for more from Will, so he adds:

Anyway, I rented it. But when I asked you yesterday if you knew of—

Glad somebody finally rented it. Folks round here sure weren't interested.

Will, thrown, retrenches:

Why not?

On account of what happened in there and all.

Will's need to know compels him to abandon his gotcha moment in favor of getting some answers:

So what happened in there?

She shrugs:

Ah honey. No sense raisin the dead. Besides, they're done and all buried now. Coffee?

Will slides his cup forward, but still wants to know:

What do you mean the dead are all buried now?

Jasmine glances around, checking to see if she can take a moment, and then leans in:

Well, if ya just gotta know, seems the last tenant in there, he went a little loopteedoo.

Loopteedoo?

And I say that with all due respect for the recently departed.

How recently departed?

Real recent. See, apparently, that fella before you bought himself a nice, new rope from Lumpy's Hardware and hung himself in there, from the highest rafters.

It's a low ceiling.

Let's just say he done the best he could with what he had, all right?

As Jasmine moves to make a new pot of coffee, Will. Obsessing, enquires further:

So how long ago was this?

Oh that must be over...couple of weeks now.

Will grimaces:

A couple of weeks?

Jasmine leans close again, conspiratorially:

But if ya wanna know the part that gets me, they say he stashed them bones from his ritual Satanic sacrifices right there under the front porch.

Will jerks back:

Ritual Satanic... Jesus.

But Will catches himself, noting the chilly glances from the senior citizens a few stools down. So he lowers his voice and leans forward to ask:

Are you kidding me?

Like I said, the whole thing was a little atrocious. But don't you worry, honey. They's just small body parts under there now.

You mean small animal body parts, right?

*All I know for sure is he left the big chunks out there in the
swamp for the maggots ta feast and fester on. So, ya hungry,
honey, cause I gotta get back to work.*

A half hour later, kneeling down on all fours, steeling
himself, Will peers under his shadowed porch steps to see a small
pile of dried, sinewy bird carcasses.

Horrified, Will rears back up, cracking his head on the first
wooden step.

Damn it!

As he rides out the sting, he see an old tow truck cruise
slowly past, its good-ol'-boy driver shooting Will the evil-eye
from behind a pair of silly-serious mirrored sunglasses.

Will, already irked, glares back, resenting this little drive-
by 'inspection'.

As the tow truck moves off, Will climbs to his feet to
notice a Calico cat dragging a dead bird across the community
grounds, bypassing all the other cottages in favor of Will's.

He then observes the cat yanking his kill under his porch to
deposit along with his other kills.

A moment later, the cat reemerges and trots back out into
the wilds for more hunting fun. A working cat.

Will's eyes roll because lord knows, he's done been had.
So he climbs back into the Chevy.

Will steps back in and returns to a seat at the counter,
where Jasmine's just serving a regular his gravy over
hushpuppies lunch.

My, gettin ta be a regular already.

Will shakes his head:

Not for long, I'm afraid.

What do ya mean?

I've decided to move on. Coffee, please.

Jasmine pauses, curious:

Move on? But ya just moved in.

It's a long story. Sorry, what was your name again?

Jasmine hesitates, but then extends her hand:

Jasmine. Jasmine Bell.

They shake.

Will Woods. How do you do?

Sometimes I do, honey, and sometimes I don't. All depends.

As Jasmine pours him a cup of coffee:

Well after what you told me, let's just say I won't.

Won't what, honey?

Live in the suicide den of some blood-lusting, Satan-worshipping killer.

Jasmine shakes her head:

Ah honey, what I told ya about them bones was just—

I don't want to talk about it, all right? But don't worry, I'm sure they'll find some other weirdo to rent it to soon enough. Just hope I can get back my deposit.

Jasmine tries again:

But, honey, all that I told ya was just—

Please, not now. If you don't mind. Enough is enough. And I've already had plenty enough, what with the accident and all!

Now Jasmine finds herself becoming a little intrigued:

What accident?

I really don't want to talk about it, all right? I don't mean to be rude but, between the TV coverage, and all the rest, I'm done.

Will slides his coffee cup forward, indicating he would like her to fill his cup again as Jasmine shrugs.

Suit yourself, darlin.

Think I could also use something to eat. A last supper so to speak, before I pack up and leave this place for good. No offense.

Jasmine allows him the dig, feeling a little guilty.

Tell ya what: on account of all your troubles, supper's on the house. Fair enough?

In the time it takes to cook a steak, Jasmine slides a fat one in front of Will, complete with all the trimmings.

He accepts this freebie with a blithe, if secret, satisfaction:

Before ya go doin any movin, Willy, ya best stop by my place later. Think we need ta clear a little somethin up.

Will nods, making sure to give her a prime view into his mouthful of masticated steak.

Sure thing.

As the evening creeps over the swamp, arriving like an old friend to the growing chirp-buzz of the ubiquitous bachelor crickets, Will steps up to Jasmine's cottage door.

But before he can knock, Jasmine opens her door wearing an old tank top and a worn pair of short denim cutoffs. Southern sexy.

As he tries to hide his surging blood pressure, she gestures at her porch chairs.

Take a load off, honey.

As Will sits, he is startled to see a spider the size of an aircraft carrier suspended on its dense web, strung between two of her porch columns.

That's...one hell of a spider.

Him? Oh he wouldn't hurt a...well, actually, he would hurt a fly. Flies and moths, mostly. But me and him, we get along just fine. Now, about what I was tellin ya the other day...

As Will listens, he finds himself lulled by the languid cadence of her soft, mesmerizing Georgia drawl.

Now, heaven knows, all drawls are alike, and if this was, say, Mississippi, the twang and curl wouldn't have had the same effect; it wouldn't have had that certain lilt, dip and soft-hip-sway that can cause a northerner, run ragged on his caffeine, to so easily melt and release into the slow-flow of an evening like this, to find himself so mystically soothed and enchanted by the hypnotizing rhythms of words.

Feeling for a time like a child dozing at his mother's breast, Will quietly rallies himself, determined to keep up his ruse a little longer by adding a dash of shock to his reply when she names the cat as the culprit:

You mean it was all... just a lie?

Not a lie exactly, honey. More like...a story.

A story?

That's right. See, storytellin's kinda a tradition down here. But we don't mean nothin by it.

Then why do you do it?

Jasmine shrugs:

Maybe on account of we got too much heat on the brain.

Will gives her a knows-better look.

Jasmine resists a moment, but then allows a small, confessional grin:

Course, that might just be a story, too, honey. Hard ta tell. Things get so mixed up down here.

Will then hears the lawyer in him counter:

But if the storyteller doesn't know the difference between what's true and what's not, how's the listener supposed to?

They're not supposed to, darlin. That's sorta the point.

Which is what makes it a lie, wouldn't you say?

Jasmine shakes her head:

No, because a lie can't tell the truth. But a story can, even if it ain't exactly true.

Will considers, offering a sly eye as he responds slowly:

Really?

She shoots right back:

Really.

They trade a competitor's knowing grin. Will then ventures:

So what's your story, Jasmine?

You first, honey.

Will smiles, entertained by her evasive ways.

All right. I came down here to...well, for one thing, to write.

Write what?

A true crime novel.

What's that?

That's where you take an actual crime and write about everything that led up to it, so it reads like a whodunit novel.

Jasmine adds:

Only by the end, everyone knows who done it, for all the world ta see?

That's the idea.

She takes another moment and then asks:

But what if the events leadin up to the crime ain't all exactly clear?

Well, then that's all just part of the mystery. But if it's done right, any good whodunit story is about something deeper than just the facts of the case.

Jasmine's eyes seem to appraise him, suddenly seeing him in a new light:

Deeper than the facts?

Any good crime novel is about getting at the real human motives and complexities that drive people even when we don't know what's driving us.

She gazes out to the swamp and then looks back to Will:

So if I understand ya correctly – and I believe I do – you gonna find yourself an actual crime, but then make a whole lotta stuff up around it so your reader don't really know what part's true, and what part's made up, all just so you can get at some deeper truth, as ya say. Is that it?

Will's about to say yes, but then realizes she's setting a trap when she adds:

In other words, Will Woods, you came down here ta tell stories just like we do?

He eyes her, disarmed to the point of feeling a little naked as her attention turns to track something crossing the grassy grounds between their cottages.

Will turns to see what she's looking at, and sees Gomer, the calico terminator cat, dragging yet another kill from the bush.

Speakin of a whodunit, here comes Gomer now. He likes ta keep a record of his conquests – ya know, the way most males of the species do? So them bones ya got under your place, we call 'em Gomer's Pile. But he don't mind where he keeps them, so all ya gotta do is get yourself a shovel and move them to wherever, and he'll...

But she stops, surprised to watch as Gomer drags the fallen bird under her porch. Jasmine considers how that could be and then turns to give Will a sly eye:

Looks like Gomer's done already taken care of that.

Will shrugs as innocently as he can:

How about that?

They eye each other again, sharing the look of two people ready to move their game to the next level.

They then lean back into her chairs to listen to the hiss and grind of the bachelor crickets searching for love – which is as much a part of the southern night as is the darkness itself.

A little ways down the highway, Sheriff Reynolds steps back into the Coroner's office to find him cleaning his scalpels.

In the background, a porcelain-covered slab supports the bloated body in question:

Well?

The coroner snorts his nose:

That there's Mason Carver.

Reynolds sobers and moves over to have another, incredulous look:

That's Mason?

What's left of him.

Reynolds shakes his head.

Now ain't that just one, big, fat coincidence?

Later that night, as Will lies in bed, unable to sleep in the oppressive, inescapable heat, he suddenly rips off the covers and lunges up, frustrated, grumbling a blue streak.

He steps outside, trying to cool himself off as the tree crickets buzz away under an alabaster moon.

As he stands there in the moonlight, he looks over to see a honey-soft light glowing from Jasmine's cottage window.

A moment later, Jasmine, naked, moves into clear view, trying to cool herself by massaging ice cubes down her creamy neck and breasts, letting the water droplets trickle down her smooth stomach as she sits by her open window.

Will halts, transfixed, riveted to the spot, unable to tear his eyes from her sensual overpowering, mesmerizing ritual – just as Jasmine, sensing something, peers out to see Will standing there.

After a suspended moment in which Will feels seared to the spot, Jasmine moves calmly out of view and turns off her light.

Will, shamed and shocked, yet feeling as if under a bewitched spell, continues to stand there a moment more, reeling helplessly.

But as the seconds tick past, his eyes close with chagrin:

Real smooth, Will. Real damn smooth.

Back at the diner the next morning, Will arrives in a hurry to fight again with door's push/pull mechanism. He finally busts in to see Jasmine standing by one of the booths, filled with locals swapping fish stories.

As they burst into laughter, Will advances, sheepish.

The table quiets as Will arrives, making him feel even more self-conscious as he tries to get Jasmine's attention.

But she gives a neutral look, turns a cool shoulder and moves off, getting back to work. So Will follows her:

I came by to say I'm sorry.

As Jasmine goes about her duties:

I couldn't sleep, so I went for a walk. And I just happened to look up and—

And kept right on lookin?

She nails him with a look then heads off to deliver a breakfast special.

Will wants to follow, so she hits him with another stern look. He retrenches to take a stool at the coffee counter.

A moment later, Jasmine comes back to make a new pot of coffee, only feet from Will.

If you'd just let me explain—

So just how long were ya standin out there playin Peepin Tom?

Only a few seconds. I swear. And I wasn't peeping.

You one of them boys who likes ta watch, honey, cause he can't handle the weight and responsibility of a full-on touch? Is that what ya are, Willy?

No! Not at all. Which is why I'm here. To say I'm sorry.

There's snakes out there at night, in the grass. But then maybe you ain't worried cause snakes don't bite they own.

As Jasmine nails Will with yet another look, Sheriff Reynolds walks into the Diner, sober and hulking. Jasmine calls over:

How ya doin, Sheriff?

Ya seen Katie lately?

Not lately. Why?

Reynolds declines to answer and then eyes Will. So Will extends his hand:

I'm Will. Will Woods.

Reynolds waits for more.

I just rented a place next to Jasmine's, as it turns out.

Satisfied, Reynolds grips Will's hand as he looks to Jasmine:

He bein a good neighbor so far?

Jasmine lets the question hang in the air for a moment, forcing Will to sweat at the delay, his hand inextricably gripped by Reynolds:

So far, Sheriff. But ya never know with men, do ya?

Will can barely contain his relief as Reynolds nods a 'good enough' and releases Will's hand back into Will's custody, offering:

You have a pleasant day now, Mr. Woods.

As Reynolds heads out again, Will turns to Jasmine thankfully. But she corners him again:

If ya wanna see me naked again, ya gonna have ta earn that, right honey?

She moves off, leaving her point all but tattooed on Will's forehead.

As Will drives back to his cottage, not feeling much better for having tried to apologize, he notices that tow truck he saw earlier gaining on him in his rear view.

Will begins to accelerate as the tow truck continues to bear down on him like a heat-seeking missile, causing Will to floor it, quickly racing his Chevy's rebuilt motor to its whining limits.

But that damn tow truck just keeps coming, faster and faster, until it's breathing down Will's bumper, about to plow him under.

So Will swerves, angling the Chevy off road to avoid being hit.

As the Chevy bucks onto the dirt shoulder, bouncing wildly along before finally breaking to a rough, dust-cloud stop, the tow truck speeds gleefully on, escaping down the highway.

Will jumps out of the Chevy, enraged:

Come back here, you sonofabitch!

But the tow truck's long gone, leaving Will standing alone by the side of the bayou highway, in the middle of nowhere, livid.

He yanks out his cell phone and tries to make a 911 call, only to get the 'no signal' alert.

Goddamnit!

Irate but stymied, Will climbs back into the Chevy and continues on his way.

As evening rolls around again, and the tree crickets begin to sing their buzzing songs, Will, having spent the afternoon at the end of the dock decompressing, starts back up to his cottage.

On the way, he passes by Jasmine and a black woman in her thirties, rocking amiably on Jasmine's porch.

Will, taking care not to be caught looking at them, suddenly hears:

Maybe he just ain't interested in women after all.

Will slows, stops and turns to see Jasmine and Katie Wells, the woman Sheriff Reynolds had been asking after. Jasmine was eyeing him with her sassy, brown eyes, her shapely body all but hidden under a conservative Baptist cotton dress.

The two women grin teasingly and seductively as Jasmine adds:

My, my, Willy, pass by two fine lookin females and ya don't even try ta steal a peek? What's that tell ya?

Will smiles warily:

Tells me I can't win for losing.

Jasmine grins as if whatever was bothering her before is now all forgiven.

Care ta join us, honey? Couple southern belles tellin stories? Unless of course ya aren't up ta that.

Will, buoyed, nods:

I'm all ears.

Jasmine purses her lips:

Ears, darlin, is a long ways up from what you are.

Will tries to suppress a surging blush as Katie volunteers:

Would ya look at that: got us a white boy turnin watermelon red.

Jasmine shrugs in agreement and gestures to Will:

This is Katie, honey.

Will nods, already down for the count:

How do you do?

Katie smiles unmistakably:

Sometimes I do. And sometimes I don't.

Will shakes his head:

Maybe I should just give up right now.

Jasmine smiles mysteriously:

Now don't be a quitter, honey. All ya need ta get along down here is an ornery, unreasonable opinion you're willin ta die for regardless of the facts. Think ya can manage that?

Jasmine's kitchen is a study in Bohemian, eclectic southern handcrafts, framed by a quaint, traditional wallpaper and long out-dated fixtures, as if she'd furnished her world in an antique shop.

As Will, Jasmine and Katie slurp down large wedges of dripping watermelon, Will tries not to notice how sexy these two women are making it look. And feel.

Or maybe it's just been too long a while since Will knew that feeling, so he tries to ground himself, sensing his own vulnerability.

At such a heated moment, some men might try reviewing baseball stats in their heads. Others might try doing multiplication tables. But Will just looks down, worried his eyes will yet be his downfall.

So ya married, Willy?

Will looks back up to see Katie eyeing him:

Divorced, for all intents and purposes.

Makes three of us. So how long since ya left your wife?

What day is it?

Katie shoots a look to Jasmine:

Uh-oh. Got us the walkin wounded.

Will feels himself straighten up in his chair:

Do I look wounded?

Jasmine checks with Katie, then replies:

Actually I'd say ya look hungry, hungry.

Will, trying to wrest back control of this conversation, spins her meaning with:

Hungry to get on with my life, if that's what you mean. Sometimes you just have to cut line.

Jasmine smiles:

Do ya?

You don't; you can end up spending your whole life looking in the rear view mirror. Not me, thanks.

Jasmine seems to take that in stride and then asks:

Any children involved?

No. You?
None that I'm aware of, as you boys like ta say.
Katie put down her slice to inquire:
So where exactly ya from, Willy?
Chicago.
Katie arches a mock brow:
A sophisticated big city boy, huh?
Nobody called me Willy, if that's what you mean.
Jasmine reflects:
Too bad. It may have been just what ya needed.
Katie then presses him gently:
So what'd ya do up Chicago-way?
Torte law.
With a straight face, Katie asks:
That anything like Walnut torte?
Not certain if she's just pulling his legs, he offers a neutral:
Not exactly.
Jasmine takes up the interview:
So you're a lawyer?
Not anymore.
Why not, you do somethin ya shouldn't have?
Yeah: I became a lawyer.
Katie leans in a little:
So what brings ya down here, Willy?
Before he can answer, Jasmine turns to Katie:
Didn't I tell ya, baby? Willy here's gonna write himself a
novel.
Katie adjusts her dress suggestively as Katie chimes in:
Ya don't say. So ya come for the local color, is that it?
Jasmine answers for Will:
Actually, he told me he come for the crime. A true crime
story ta write about.
Katie feigns romantic disappointment:
So which is it, Willy? The color? Or the crime?
They both look to him, apparently eager for his answer, so
he offers:
Both, actually. And also for some…personal reasons, too.
Jasmine takes special note of that:
What personal reasons, Willy?

Personal as in personal reasons.

Jasmine smiles, apparently somehow reassured by his rebuff.

As the moment hangs in the air, leaving only silence in its wake, Jasmine suddenly spins the conversation back in her direction:

Well if it's local color you're after, ya can't beat old Hank Boyd. Now he's some local color alright. Ol' Hank used ta be Okefenokee's very own exterminator.

Katie smiles and leans back at the thought of Hank, fanning herself as Jasmine continues:

See Ol' Hank, he liked to exterminatin things, and I mean everythin from bugs ta snakes ta ya-name-it. Now Hank was also what ya might call the quiet type. But one day while mixin them toxic brews of his, he sorta burnt his biscuit. Next thing we know, Ol' Hank's exterminatin the whole town in his birthday suit. I don't know whether them bugs left on account of Hank's sprayin, or on account of seein Hank the way God made him, but leave they did. And for one whole summer we was certifiably bug-free. Course, ya couldn't drink the water, but that's another story.

As he listens, Will imagines a small town of drop-jawed onlookers eyeing Hank, a lithe, wild sixties, butt naked, prancing about like a latter-day Tinker Bell with a tin canister strapped to his back as Jasmine turns to Katie:

How about a true-crime for Willy? Can ya think of one?

Katie thinks and then smiles:

Sonny Billings.

Jasmine has to smile:

Sonny. Lord. What was that, bout five years back? Anyway, seems Sonny decides he's tired of his girlfriend. Only instead of cuttin line as you put it, Sonny buys hisself a knife. And he cuts that poor child up inta these little tiny pieces – the way ya might do cheese wedgees at a barbecue? He then stuffs them pieces into a spankin new set of picklin jars and stores her out back in the shed.

In his mind's eye, Will imagines a uniformed officer finding the jars and gagging when he suddenly recognizes their contents...as Jasmine continues:

And that's where they found her. Right next ta last summer's melon rinds. I just hope nobody mistook one for the other at one of Sonny's summer barbeques, if ya see what I mean.

Will winces, appalled but fascinated:

So why'd he store them where they'd be found?

Honey, if stupid was a crime down here, half the people I know would be on Death Row.

Just then, a pair of headlights sweep across Jasmine's kitchen wall.

Katie instantly slips down out of view as Jasmine jumps up to have a wary look at who it might be.

Then satisfied the coast's clear, Jasmine subtly signals Katie, who slides back up as if nothing happened.

Will watches all this, beguiled, as Jasmine focuses on Will again:

So if ya find the right story, Willy, ya definitely gonna write it?

Absolutely.

Then you're gonna get it published for the whole world ta see, right?

That's the plan. Why?

Jasmine trades a look with Katie:

Just wanna know if you're serious.

Am I serious?

He has to shake his head:

Ever since I can remember, all I ever wanted to do was to write. But then I started listening to all those people who tell you how you'll starve, how I needed a fall-back plan, so I end up in law school. And before I knew it I'd graduated, joined a cushy law firm and married a coed with a pretty smile. Which, these many years later, I come to find out was her best quality. Which is why two weeks ago I quit my law firm, donated everything I owned to charity, got in my Chevy and drove here with one suitcase, a laptop computer and no future to speak of. Am I serious? As a heart attack.

Jasmine and Katie eye him with a dark satisfaction, as if he's passed muster.

They trade and look; then Jasmine leans back, eyeing him in her wily way:

Then that makes three of us, honey.

Will eyes Jasmine, wondering what she means as the southern night closes in on them, humid and dark and deep with secrets.

The next morning, grey and misty under heavy humid clouds, Sheriff Reynolds paces the muddy embankment of Mason's crime scene as Officer Hales reads from his notes:

Mason left Bubba's round one. After that, nobody seen him.
Oh somebody seen him. Just like Cassius before him.

Reynolds starts up from the banks, kicking off the sticky mud.

Two boys meet their maker in the same, damn way? And what do they got in common?

Officer Hale waits for more, so Reynolds continues:
Katie and Jasmine.

As the clock creeps towards noon, still under grey, ponderous skies, Will visits the local library, sorting through stacks of old, sepia-toned newspapers, drawing suspicious looks from locals who don't like the idea of a stranger digging into their collective past.

Will finally shoots one of his silent critics with a testy look back, tiring of the curious glances coming his way, and then he hears a pleasant query:

So how's the new place workin out?

Will turns to see Dewey, balancing an arm-load of books.
Fine, thanks. What're all those for?
You're lookin at the President of the local chapter of the Nature Conservancy.
Good for you.
Not really. Truth be told, it's a royal pain in the ass. But it's good for my soul, so…what the hell. I hear you're lookin for true crime.

Will's surprised:
Wow. Word travels fast around here.
You can forget about your texts and tweets down here, friend, cause we still use the fastest form of communication known ta man:

Which is?

Dewey smiles like it's obvious:

Gossip! Speakin of which, Jasmine tell ya anythin about herself?

Not really. Why?

If crime's what you're lookin for, ya best talk ta Jasmine. But don't tell her I said so.

As Dewey moves off, Will watches after him, intrigued.

Then, gathering up his own notes, Will walks to the elevator. Seeing one open and waiting, he hurries up to catch it just as its doors begin to close.

But then a walking cane thrusts sharply into the breach, preventing the doors from closing.

As they buck back open, Will arrives to find a man, seventy years young, dressed in a rumpled-dapper linen suit donning a straw, silk-brimmed hat, but with eyes like old razors.

This is Clarence Hollister, a patriarch who seems to have strolled out of a previous time to stake and defend his claim in this one.

Will starts:

Thank you.

Not at all.

The elevator doors close them in and the car begins its creeping, lugubrious descent to the first floor, drawing a snicker from Hollister.

It's a slow ride down, like everythin else down here. Wouldn't ya say?

Will smiles pleasantly enough, but avoids the question's snare.

A few beats later, the elevator dings and its doors buck back open to reveal the ground floor. As they step off:

Ya must be new in town.

Will pauses to answer:

How'd you know?

I like ta keep on top of what goes on in my town. Good day, suh.

Hollister tips his hat and strides off onto his floor. Will watches after him, wondering if he just met the Mayor.

Back at the cottages, Will drives up in his Chevy to see Gomer dragging yet another kill under Jasmine's porch.

Minutes later, as Will shovels Gomer's pile into a wheelbarrow to move it again, that certain tow truck drives up and, this time, it parks.

Will instantly braces as Wheeler Biggs, a stocky, tattooed, hard-living thirties climbs out. He swaggers over, oozing menace, reeking of beer.

And just what da ya think you're doin?

Will readies, but plays it cool as Wheeler continues:

Who the hell said you could do Jasmine's chores for her?

Come after me in that truck again, pal, and you're going to need somebody to do your chores for you.

Wheeler shakes his head like that was the wrong damn answer.

Looks like my chore's gonna be kickin your Yankee butt!

As Wheeler puffs himself up, ready to brawl, they hear:

Goddamnit, Wheeler Biggs, I told ya never ta come round here no more!

Taken off-guard, they both turn to see Moo Moo, a big, black 60's woman in a pink Moo Moo, standing on her cottage's porch across the way, angry as a swarm of hornets:

Wheeler, trying to look tough, yells:

Shut up, bitch!

He then turns back to Will, ready to rumble.

Now, where was I?

As Will grips the shovel, ready to defend himself, a sudden shotgun blast compels their attentions once more back to Moo Moo, now holding a shotgun with the confidence of someone who knows how to use it:

This bitch is in a bad mood, Wheeler. So ya really wanna try yo luck?

Wheeler sobers and then tries to downplay things:

We's just talkin, Moo Moo.

I said get, Wheeler! And I mean now if ya wanna make it ta supper!

She cocks the shotgun, ejecting the spent shell for emphasis.

27

So Wheeler's forced to retreat, but he spits at Will under his breath:

Jasmine's mine! Ya hear?

Moo Moo fires off another round, spraying the grass near Wheeler's feet, at which he high-tails back to his truck, jumps in and speeds away.

Will, not knowing what comes next, turns slowly to Moo Moo, who shrugs matter-of-factly:

They call me Moo Moo.

Will. Woods.

Moo Moo nods, ejects the spent cartridge onto her porch and walks calmly back into her cottage as though this was all in a day's work.

Will exhales, trying to coax his blood pressure back down as Gomer, unperturbed, trots past him, heading back out into the wilds to continue the hunt.

That night, as Jasmine finally pulls back up to her cottage, she finds Will waiting for her on her porch, seated in one of her chairs, looking none too pleased.

Somethin the matter, honey?

Who the hell is Wheeler Biggs? Or should I say: what the hell is Wheeler Biggs?

Jasmine shrugs with a certain concern:

He come around here again?

Apparently it's what he lives to do.

Jasmine ponders and then says:

Walk and talk?

As they stroll, watching the moonlight dance on the black waters of Okefenokee, Jasmine asks:

Wheeler didn't go botherin ya, did he?

No bother. I like guys who want to tear my head off.

Well all I can say is he just better be careful.

He should?

On account of his probation and all.

Probation? Perfect. For what?

That's kinda a long story, honey.

Will can't help but roll his eyes:

And this is your boyfriend?
Is that what he said?
He practically peed a circle around your porch!
Well, considerin all that beer he guzzles, I bet he could.
Fact, I bet he could manage two and half circles.*

Will sneers, dripping sarcasm:
What a guy! So are you?
Am I what, darlin?
His girlfriend?

Jasmine slows:
Let's just say I may have had a little too much to drink one very unfortunate night, and leave it at that. All right?

Will grimaces with a certain disappointment, which Jasmine sees, and it affects her more than she'd care to admit.

Well, it's not like I don't regret it each and every single day of my life, believe me. And if ya wanna know the real tragic part, I thought I'd gone home with someone else. So just imagine my surprise the mornin after.

That's a very touching story, Jasmine. Except for one detail: if it was such a mistake, why the hell haven't you told him to just get lost?

Jasmine seems unperturbed by the question. In fact, as Will eyes her, she seems more saddened by it all than concerned:
No need to, honey. Sooner or later, he'll up and vanish. Just like they all do.

Just like all who do?

She eyes him like its obvious:
Men.

What about men?

They vanish, honey. Even the ones ya don't want to, one day they just eventually vanish.

Will balks:
Oh I see. So it's all our fault. And women are all just a bunch of victim-virgin saints. Is that it?

All I'm sayin is women don't vanish.

Could've fooled me.

But the look in Jasmine's eye compels him to ask her again:
So what, in your opinion, do women do?

Women? We just fade away, honey. Even before we're
gone, we're gone.

As Will absorbs that, struck by the truth in her observation,
Jasmine strolls on ahead.

Later, as Will and Jasmine walk back up the road together,
back to the cottages, they find Katie sitting on Jasmine's porch,
looking concerned:
Well, hello, honey. Didn't expect ta see ya tonight.
Katie gets up:
Thought of another crime story you could tell Willy.
Oh? And which one would that be?
You know the one.
Jasmine slows, her eyes suddenly diving into Katie's, who
looks back knowingly.

Will and Katie are sitting around the kitchen table again as
Jasmine grabs a few beers from her fridge, letting Katie do the
set-up:
Could take a few sittins to tell, Willy.
I'm game.
Yet Jasmine doesn't seem so game, and looks over at Katie
at she sits back down at the table.
Katie responds by taking a beer and cracking one open for
Jasmine, as Jasmine looks to be still making up her mind.
So Katie urges her again:
Come on, honey. About time it was told.
As the night gives way to the saw of the bachelor crickets,
Will waits, wondering why Jasmine's hesitating.
But then Jasmine finally turns to him with that raw but wily
gaze of hers:
Know what an object of desire is, Willy?
An object of desire can mean different things to different
people.
That's right. It sure can. But on this particular occasion,
the object of desire was a bullfrog...
Before long, Will can see Jasmine's story playing out
before him in his mind's eyes, beginning with a fat bullfrog
croaking on a small islet as a ten year old boy, his face smudged

with mud, creeps out onto a flimsy limb, wholly focused on catching that bullfrog.

And the desiree was a boy named Gabe, who done got himself up a tree...

Will listens as Jasmine describes how…

Gabe, armed with a homemade sling shot, slides farther and farther out onto the branch, angling for a clear sling-shot at that bullfrog.

Finally arriving at the spot, balancing himself, he readies his sling shot, only to hear a nearby splash.

When he looks to see what caused it, he pales at the sight of a huge alligator slithering through the waters, moving to position itself under his drooping branch.

Panicking, Gabe tries to slide back down the branch, but as he moves, the branch cracks under his weight and dips sharply towards the swamp.

Gabe grabs on for dear life, digging in his nails into its bark as his feet dangle just above the alligator's jaws.

Rallying, Gabe hoists himself back up, just as the alligator snaps at his feet. Escaping for the moment, he hangs there terrified and marooned, unable to rescue himself.

So he cries out:

Help! Can anybody hear me?

As Gabe's fingers begin to lose their tenuous grip, he tries to pull himself up again, but the branch cracks more, dropping him even closer to the alligator's waiting jaws.

As tears stream from Gabe's terrified eyes, he hears a man's voice calling:

Gabe? Son?

Dad? Dad!

Gabe?

I'm here, Dad!

Orlando suddenly bounds out of the bush like Errol Flynn. He's a dashing 30's, with daring eyes and an athlete's body. Reacting instantly, Orlando picks up a rock, takes careful aim and flings it at the gator, striking it flush in the side. The gator flinches and slithers away, allowing Orlando to wade out into the swamp, where Gabe can slide down off the branch into the safety of Orlando's arms.

He then carries Gabe to safety as Gabe's body relaxes into his father's strong, reassuring arms...

Will, reacting to a break in her story, looks up to find Jasmine momentarily lost in thought. When she realizes Will is waiting for more, she continues:

You could say his father was all any boy could ever wish for. But he was also more than any boy could handle.

As Gabe, Orlando and Megan, Gabe's soulful mother, with long hair and fragile eyes, eat their modest dinner together, relaxed, enjoying each other, an unexpected knock sets Megan on edge.

She looks at Orlando, imploring him to keep his promise.

But as another knock rattles the room, Gabe jumps up and moves to the door, cautiously opening it to find a crooked old man, his spine bent by time, but his eyes full of a predator's vitality:

Why you must be Gabe?

As he feels a chill making the hairs on the back of his little neck stand up, the man adds:

I've heard so much about ya, son. My friends call me Crebbs.

What do ya want?

My? Straight ta business. I like that in a man. I have a small matter ta transact with yo daddy.

Orlando steps up behind Gabe. Crebbs' eyes shift and bore into Orlando's, exerting an unspoken control.

Orlando pushes past Gabe and goes outside, closing the door behind him.

Gabe then turns back to see his mother's look of dread, and a sudden need to do something, to somehow save the day overcomes him – which is why moments later Gabe sneaks into the barn to see Orlando, transformed by Crebbs' moonshine, quickly becoming the vitriolic drunk of Gabe's nightmares.

Crebbs, about to seal a large sale, spots Gabe and snaps:

Get outta here! Ya hear me?

Orlando turns, sees Gabe and heaves an empty bottle at him.

As Gabe ducks away, the bottle shatters against the barn door in his wake.

Later, Gabe and his mom huddle together, terrified by the violent stranger Orlando becomes when he drinks. They know he is about to make his return from the barn as they can hear his slurring rants in the night, laying waste anything and everything in his way.

Meghan grips Gabe all the more tightly, admonishing him:

If that man ever comes here askin for yo father again, ya tell him ya don't know where he's at, understand? Never let that man know where yo Daddy's at!

Gabe nods, promising, guilty.

But as Orlando's rants continue, threatening any who would defy him, Gabe can't endure them any more and, escaping from his mother's arms, lunges up and runs out.

Gabe, come back here!

But Gabe runs away, wondering if he'll ever come back, making his way along the banks of the swamp, angling for his secret hiding place.

As he runs, he hears something rustling on the opposite banks and, alarmed, whips around to see . . .

Just then, a pair of headlights illumine Jasmine's kitchen wall, halting her tale and causing her to quickly get up and peer warily out the window as Katie slides down again, out of view:

Guess who's here, darlin.

Katie instantly moves to sneak out the back door as Will looks on, confused but piqued.

Jasmine admonishes Will:

Let me do the talkin, honey.

A moment later, Sheriff Reynolds's hulking shadow fills Jasmine's screen door.

That you, Sheriff?
Where's she at, Jasmine?
Not here. As ya can see.

Reynolds pauses a skeptical beat, then orders:

Well, when you do see her, tell her the fella we found out in the swamp is Mason.

Jasmine sobers:

Mason?

You heard me. Which is why I'm gonna need ta speak ta Katie. And ta you.

Jasmine instantly objects:

Me? Why me?

Let's just say for old time's sake.

Reynolds lingers a moment more and then steps off, retreating back into the night.

A few beats later, Will hears Reynolds's cruiser start up and drive slowly away into the night.

As Will looks to Jasmine, Katie creeps back through the back door to rejoin them at Jasmine's kitchen table.

She looks preoccupied and shaken, so Will turns to Jasmine:

What was that all about?

Jasmine considers his question and then offers:

Mason was Katie's husband. Well, ex-husband. Ex everythin now, I guess.

Will waits for more, but instead, Jasmine gets up and opens her cottage door, signaling it's time to go:

That's all the storytelling for tonight, Willy.

Will gets up and leaves with a nod, sensing a world of stories he's never likely to hear as Jasmine locks her door behind him.

Later that sweltering night, as Will tosses and turns, unable to sleep, a car motor starts up outside, beckoning his attention.

Will slides from bed and peeks out his window to see Jasmine and Katie driving off together into the night…

The next morning, as Will lies prostrate on top of his bed covers, looking like a car wreck victim, a shrill ring shocks his attention back to his cellphone.

Hello? That you, Jim?

After listening to Jim a bit, Will's blood pressure surges, and he gets up to pace as he reaffirms his position.

No, Jim, I expect you to bury her. Alive. No mercy. ...Well she damn well put herself in this position, literally, the bitch! And now she's going to pay the piper.

Jim tries to talk him down, but Will's not having it:

I am too dealing with it. You look back in life, Jim, you turn into a pillar of dung! So I'm cutting line on Brenda. ...Would you stop trying to play psychologist and concentrate on being my lawyer, please?...Look, just screw my wife and send me the paperwork, okay?

Just then, Will sees Moo Moo walking past his door, scowling at what she's just overheard. So he continues in a strident whisper:

Just do it, goddamnit!

Back in town, Will walks into the barren foyer of the city hall to find a civil servant lady at her small desk. The musty place is otherwise empty.

I'd like to have a look at your vital statistics records, please.

What for?

If you must know, I'm interested in somebody who might've lived here 30 years ago.

The civil servant lady looks him over suspiciously and then sees his cellphone:

You can't go in there with that.

This is a phone, lady.

And a camera, and a recordin device, if I'm not mistaken, which makes it against the law.

Those are public records in there?

Do ya wanna see them or not?

Although he is unwilling to obey, he hands over his phone as the lady moves to unlock the records room door.

Will enters to find a small, crypt-like enclosure, piled sloppily from floor to ceiling with thick, dusty, handwritten files.

As she parts, the lady warns:

If you move, or remove one of them files, you'll go to jail.

As the day creeps past, Will is sitting at the room's cramped metal desk, pouring over the files. Then he hears the door open and turns to see Clarence Hollister, dressed in his linen suit, hat and cane, step in.

So. We meet again, suh.

Will, instantly suspicious, nods:

So we do.

Hollister takes another step forward and has himself a look around. Then:

I understand you're interested in lookin up someone who might've lived here some 30 years back.

And your interest would be?

Maybe I can help. I've known just about everybody who's ever lived here for the past 60 years. So, who exactly ya lookin for?

Will tries to demur:

It's nothing, really, but thanks anyway, Mr.—

Hollister. Clarence T. the third, at your service.

Hollister moves to Will. Extends a bony hand. They shake.

Will Woods. The first. Far as I know.

Like they say, there's a first time for everythin.

Will endures the witless quip, sensing it's all part of some blustery charm offensive about to reveal its true intent:

So what brings ya to our fair swamp, Mr. Woods?

Call it a vacation.

A vacation? And ya mean ta waste it in a dark little crypt like this?

Will, not fooled, can see right through to Hollister's visit:

These are public records, are they not, Mr. Hollister?

But of course they are, Mr. Woods. Open for one and all ta see, regardless of race, creed or color. It's just that…

Just that what, Mr. Hollister?

As Mayor of this town – did I mention I was Mayor? – I take a special interest in protectin the good name of my constituents. Be they livin, or be they dead.

I'll keep that in mind.

You do that, Mr. Woods. You do that.

Will's courtroom instincts kick in and he resists comment, letting a silence fall so as to not offer Hollister any new openings to engage him or continue his uninvited visit.

So Hollister tips his hat and starts for the door, but then turns:

Oh. By the way: are ya perchance related to Jasmine Bell?

Why do you ask?

I understand ya been spendin some time with her.

Is that a matter of public record, too?

No, suh. Except that if ya ain't related by blood, then I feel it my duty ta inform ya that Ms. Bell – or should I say 'Anastasia Jasmine Mae Bell' – has, of her own free will, led a regrettable life of dubious character. A life ya might want ta acquaint yourself with before ya go riskin your good name around town, if ya see what I mean.

Will responds neutrally:

As I said, I'll keep it in mind, Mr. Mayor.

Then I believe I've done my neighborly duty here. Good day to ya, suh.

As Hollister exits, Will watches after him, more amazed and incredulous than threatened.

That evening, back at Jasmine's kitchen table, Will cracks open a couple of beers, lost in thought.

Jasmine eyes him, sensing his preoccupation:

Somethin on your mind, Willy?

So how's Katie doing?

Fine. Why?

I take it she didn't like Mason much?

Time was she liked him enough ta marry him.

Will waits for more:

She just wasn't too keen on gettin beat up all the time. Katie's kinda particular that way.

I'm sorry. I didn't know.

An awkward silence falls, so Will tries another tack:

That Mayor of yours is quite a character.

Jasmine's eyes suddenly rivet:

What did he want?

Wanted to know if we were related.

Related? And what did you say?
I said that it wasn't any of his business.
Jasmine stares at Will, suspiciously:
Ya sure that's all you told him?
Yes.
But Jasmine's eyes continue to bore into his:
What, Jasmine?
You ever talk to that man again, Willy, don't bother comin round here no more cause I ain't gonna talk ta you. Ya got that? Is that clear?
Will bristles a bit at such a threat:
Excuse me?
Ya heard me.
Hey, he talked to me, okay?
I'm just gonna say this once, Willy, so listen good: ya talk to that man again, I ain't never, ever gonna talk ta you again, much less tell ya my stories. Understood?
Will stares at Jasmine, stunned as Jasmine lights up an agitated cigarette, her fingers trembling with fury.
Ya wanna hear more of the story or not, Willy?
It's 'Will'. And yes, I would.
Their eyes are locked, filled with frustration, agitation and anger – but also with an electric, explosive passion, suddenly surging.
Will feels himself angling closer to her, wanting to kiss her when Jasmine suddenly withdraws:
In that case, 'Will', would ya care ta sit down?
Will reigns in his advance, draws a subtle breath, riding out his cresting blood pressure, and sits, as Jasmine does the same:
Now. Where was I?

As Jasmine continues her story, Will imagines her words in his mind, seeing Gabe walking warily down by the swamp in the dark when he hears some rustling.
Gabe whips around to see Jojo, a small Black Boy, Gabe's age, standing on the opposite banks of the swamp, eyeing Gabe.
They look across at each other under the moon, an intuitive empathy instantly bonding them, as Jasmine describes:

If a picture's worth a thousand words, then them boys
talked a whole book in a heart beat.

But then Jojo's eyes flare, reacting in horror to something he sees near Gabe, so Gabe turns to see a large, hulking, shadowy figure emerging from the wilds, lumbering out of the grasses and onto the road, apparently as yet unaware of Gabe.

Gabe quickly hides, feeling his heart pound in his chest, and watches as the dark outline straightens itself, silhouetted against the moon, revealing itself to be an alligator standing itself up on its hind legs and tail.

As Gabe's face tightens with horror, the figure suddenly shape-shifts into Crebbs, into his angular and harsh features.

A moment later, now a full man, Crebbs shakes off the metamorphosis and strides off up the road, his tail coat flapping behind him in place of a tail, his gnarled body alive with a determined, evil vitality.

Gabe watches after him and then glances back to see Jojo.

But Jojo's gone.

So Gabe looks back after Crebbs, suddenly feeling compelled to follow...

Keeping a safe distance, Gabe tracks Crebbs deeper and deeper into the swampy wilds under an arching moon, until he watches him arrive at an old wood swamp shack.

As Crebbs goes inside, Gabe digs into his pockets and pulls out a match book. He eyes the matches and the tinderbox shack, suddenly getting an incendiary idea.

A moment later, Gabe crawls stealthily under his wooden porch steps, as quietly as he can and then strikes the match.

But just as it flares to life, he hears Crebbs step out onto the porch.

Gabe instantly snuffs out the match and freezes as Crebbs paces just above him, his heels clicking, creaking across the rotted wooden slats:

I know you're out there, boy. And I got somethin I wanna show ya. Somethin ya should see. That is, if you're man enough.

Crebbs looks around, scanning the woods with his hungry, predatory eyes as Gabe, holding his breath, lies frozen right under

Crebbs' heels...until Crebbs finally walks back inside, leaving Gabe so shaken that all he can do is run.

Feeling that Crebbs is chasing him, he dodges helter-skelter through brush and mud and tall grass, desperate to escape, constantly looking over his shoulder when he suddenly smashes into someone, causing both of them to tumble to the ground, arms and legs akimbo.

Terrorized, Gabe scrambles to untangle himself, only to discover a girl, about his age, but with haunted eyes.

She reacts slowly, finally looking up at Gabe as if she's been expecting him.

But all Gabe manages is to apologize:

I, uh, didn't mean to...

But the girl just stares at Gabe, her eyes filling with a dark promise Gabe doesn't understand, but which excites him:

Who are you?

She smiles strangely, as though she knows a salacious secret:

I'm Gabe.

...Chastity.

She moves to rub up against Gabe, thrilling him beyond his years. She then leans in as if she's about to kiss him, when the girl suddenly recoils inexplicably, spinning Gabe's emotions like a top:

What?

He's watchin.

Gabe looks around, alarmed to see nothing but tall grass:

Who's watchin?

I can feel him!

Gabe looks around again, confused, vicariously frightened.

Meet me here tomorrow night.

Meet you here?

And bring somethin nasty for us ta drink!

Chastity hurries off, disappearing into the tall grass.

A moment later, we hear a swamp crane cry out in the darkness of the night.

As Gabe finally arrives back at his cabin home, he hears someone crying inside his house.

Gabe tiptoes to a window and peers in to discover Megan, his mother, sobbing. As she moves to pull back her hair, Gabe sees her black, swollen eye.

Reigniting with rage against his father, Gabe turns and moves towards the tool shed.

Entering, he finds his father still sprawled out on the floor in a drunken stupor. Beyond him lies a wooden crate full of moonshine, and Gabe's mind screws itself to its purpose.

Retrieving a club-like branch just outside the tool shed, Gabe re-enters, resolute, and, raising the club, advances on Orlando...only to then move past him and continue on to the crate of moonshine.

Hoisting the club, he brings it down with all his might, smashing the bottles one after another in succession, exhausting himself until there's only one left.

Faltering, sweating and trembling, Gabe picks up that last bottle, eyes it and then, overwhelmed by guilt, hides it away in his pocket and slinks back out of the shed.

Emerging back out into the night, Gabe stops for a moment, unhinged, gripping the moonshine bottle now as though it was his own addiction.

Now Will hears Jasmine say:

He could've killed the 'gator that was eatin his father alive. He could've carried his father off ta safety on his shoulders, but he didn't. And he didn't know why he didn't. All he knew was he shoulda smashed them bottles from here ta Kingdom Come! But he didn't.

As Gabe runs off again, disappearing into the mists of Will's mind, he looks up, drifting back into the present to find Jasmine staring off as if she too has been seeing the events unfold before here eyes.

But then she suddenly stands up, breaking the spell, and moves to the sink to pat some cool water on her face.

Will steals a long, lingering look at Jasmine's shape and the small of her back, until Jasmine turns, catches him looking at her body, but seems to allow it. Then she says:

But even if he had smashed all the bottles, wouldn't his father have simply bought more? I mean he's an alcoholic, right? Anyway, point is, Gabe didn't smash 'em when he could've.

With his mind now more on Jasmine than her story, he nevertheless tries to reengage it:

So, then why didn't he smash them?

Because deep down, Gabe didn't want ta smash the somethin in himself that them bottles had come to represent.

And that would be?

The somethin we all got deep down in us, honey. The somethin that secretly likes what's wrong with this world; that likes ta pamper evil, cause we think it'll keep us safe from our own devils.

Later that night, as Will lies on his bed staring at a hole in the ceiling, he tries to make sense of Jasmine's story, of why she might be telling it, of why she hesitated to tell it, when he hears Jasmine's Rambler starting up.

Lunging from bed, Will moves to his window to see her Rambler drive away into the night...

The next thing Will knows, someone's knocking loudly on his door. He cracks an eye to see the morning light, and lumbers painfully from bed.

Staggering to the door, he opens it to find Moo Moo, looking annoyed, holding a fed ex envelope for him.

Damn delivery boy couldn't find his butt if it was on fire!

She pushes the envelope at him, and he nods:

Thanks.

Shut up.

Gathering himself, Will walks out and down to the dock to see the silver-dappled waters shifting shapes and hues under the changing clouds.

Feeling as if he already needs a shower in the oppressive humidity, he sits on the dock's edge and opens the envelope to find a settlement document, accompanied by a note scrawled across the top from Jim, saying: 'You won. She's screwed. Sign these and it's over. '

He stares at the documents, suddenly conflicted, which is not how he expected to feel.

Looking down past the documents, down to the muddy banks below him, he sees a small community of tiny fiddler crabs, about the size of a woman's palm, each armed with a comically large claw, and one tragically small claw.

As Will watches, a fiddler crab scurries from its hole, smacks an innocent neighbor crab for no apparent reason and then hurries back into its hole.

Then the 'smacked' crab, unable to revenge himself on the first crab, moves off to smack a third crab passing by, which, in turn, smacks yet another innocent victim.

Will watches, intrigued. Something about this misplaced game of retribution seems strangely familiar, strangely personal, strangely like the documents he's holding in his hands, when he hears:

Care ta take in some local color?

Will turns to find Jasmine, lovely in flowered cotton dress, smiling playfully – totally unlike the Jasmine of last night.

Minutes later, Will finds himself in her Rambler, speeding along a narrow strip of highway, banked by dense woods.

As the sun begins to break through the clouds, brightening the afternoon, Jasmine looks over and asks:

So how come ya never say nothin about your wife?

Because she's my ex-wife. How come you never say anything about your ex husband?

Because he's dead.

Will does a double-take:

How?

Murdered.

As Will's face registers his amazement, Jasmine returns to:

So ya love her?

Who?

Your wife!

Like I said: it's over.

Sayin it's over don't make it over, Willy.

Will holds up the divorce papers:

These do. The moment I sign them.

Jasmine knows better:

In other words: she left you.

No. I left her. Speaking of which, how's your boyfriend?

She dismisses his implied dig with a shrug.

I told ya: Wheeler's not my boyfriend.

So then it's all over between you, is it?

More over than signin a bunch of papers is gonna make it over!

Before Jasmine can enjoy her victory of sorts, her eyes suddenly focuses with concern on something up ahead:

Except that right now I need you ta get down, honey.

Excuse me?

I said get down. Now.

Though confused, Will obliges and ducks down out of sight below the dashboard just as Jasmine smiles and waves up at Wheeler racing past in his tow truck, heading in the opposite direction.

Soon Will rises back into view, his face smearing with a gotcha smirk, glances back at Wheeler's disappearing truck, and then addresses Jasmine:

Over, huh? Could I get you to sign something to that effect?

As he waits for Jasmine's come-back, her jaw tightens, but then eases into a sly grin:

Do you as bout as much good as you signin them divorce papers is doin me, darlin.

They trade a knowing look, suddenly coming to a whole new set of terms:

So are we like on a date? Is this a date, Jasmine Mae Bell?

She shrugs:

Not necessarily.

So then what is this?

All I know for sure is that someway-anuther, we seem ta got each other by the hind legs, don't we?

By the hind legs...?

So?

So I'm just trying to picture that.

Will grins over, and Jasmine cracks up, and they continue along on their way, on their not-necessarily-a-date day of local color...which turns out to be Aunt Viv's place.

Picture an old, prefab house set on elevated stilts, surrounded by wild grasses, banked by a dense growth of trees and smelling of clay and weeds.

As they pull up and park, they find a gathering of old folks sitting in a circle, including wives in faded, floral cotton dresses and husbands in armpit-stained, short-sleeved shirts with suspendered pants, all sitting in a circle in a fence-less yard.

Jasmine walks Will up to the circle:

Aunt Viv, everyone, this is Willy. Willy Woods. He's from Chicago.

Will nods to everyone:

How do you do?

Everybody nods pleasantly back as Will and Jasmine pull up folding chairs to join the serene circle.

Will glances around, waiting for something to happen, for someone to say something, anything, but everyone seems content to just sit there while a few fan themselves.

Only the whir of a Swamp Cooler can be heard as the afternoon stretches out around them as if it, too, was ready for a long nap.

Will looks around amazed and perplexed at first, and then lulled and comforted by the long pauses between words, between topics of conversation, between any utterances at all, save for the fact that they are all there, seated in a circle, keeping each other as they mark these moments by simply being together.

For a city boy like Will, the art of it, the audacity of it and the shear serenity of it arrive to his slowly awakening awareness like a revelation.

Later, as the afternoon takes that nap around them, Aunt Viv, fanning herself with a paper plate, shakes her head:

My. It's hotter than a firecracker lit at both ends and poppin in the middle.

Everyone nods their considered agreement, drawn back from their distant thoughts. Then they all retreat back into their own private worlds, re-submerging into the quiet of a restful afternoon.

Will glances around, bemused, succumbing to their pace, their endless patience.

Maybe an hour later, one of the old men looks up to say:

George Riley got hisself a new truck.

One of the women responds:

He did?

Which allows the old man to add:

A blue one. Real nice.

Everyone again nods their approval as Will waits for someone else to jump in, to add some further detail, to volunteer some other new development around town.

But no one does, and Will hears himself say:

A blue one, huh?

The old man nods, and the silence settles in again like an old dog curling up to sleep.

Later still, Will, dozing in the humid air, begins to tip over slowly towards Jasmine, but she elbows just enough so that he sits up, flinching back to consciousness.

Worried he's made a scene, he glances around to find no one is paying him any mind, and the marvel of it all begins to dawn on him because nothing here seems out of bounds, forbidden or taboo, and no one needs to impress.

As the evening seeps over Aunt Viv's place like deepening shades of watercolor hues, Jasmine and Will bid their goodbyes, and then Jasmine drives Will home. On the way, Will stares out the window, occasionally flaring his facial muscles to wake himself.

Jasmine looks over and inquires:

So ya have a nice time, Willy?

Yes. Except for a while there I couldn't remember what day it was.

Jasmine smiles:

That's the point, darlin. That's a genuine southern visit, where what ya say don't matter much, but bein there counts for everythin.

As Will considers that, Jasmine suddenly veers the Rambler down an old, dirt road that leads into a thickly wooded grove, off the beaten track, to buck along the shady, back road:

Where're we going?

To another time and place, honey.

Jasmine drives out into the clearing and parks the Rambler.

They climb out to see a stretch of serene beauty – blue-green waters, endless savanna grasses and an abandoned, weather-beaten house, partially burned, overlooking it all.

What is this place?

Home. Least for one more week it is. Most folks now call it the 'Pinch' on account of it bein pinched in between them two big oil claims we got on either side.

As Will watches her stroll on ahead, he sees again just how beautiful she is – the breeze in her honey hair, her knowing, sad eyes – and a sudden rush of desire for her surges through his body.

She turns just in time to catch the look on his face.

She knows the look, but plays innocent:

What, Willy?

Is this where you come at night?

Keepin an eye on me, are ya?

Not a very good one if I have to ask where you go at night.

She smiles, amused, secretly glad he cares:

Here, mostly. While I still can. Until the tax man takes it.

Why?

Back taxes.

So sell it. What are you waitin for? No doubt the oil companies would buy it.

Jasmine sneers:

No doubt.

I'm serious. You might even end up making a profit after taxes.

But she doesn't seem interested, so Will pursues her, feeling like a lawyer again:

You hearing me on this?

She turns:

Are you hearing me? This is my home, Willy. My heart. I don't intend ta sell my heart if that's all right with ya.

Will stares at her, stymied by her strange logic:

Unless you owe back taxes on your heart, Jasmine, at this point, if I understand you correctly, you don't have a better option.

Jasmine softly smiles to herself:

It's one thing ta be a lawyer, Willy. It's another ta have a lawyer for a heart.

But before Will can argue, they hear a car and turn to see Reynolds rolling up in his cruiser.

As Will braces, Jasmine shifts gears back into her wily waitress ways:

Keepin an eye on things, Sheriff?

If Katie don't come ta see me on her own, Jasmine, I'm gonna have ta come get her.

And exactly how would that be any different from most times?

Reynolds' eyes storm:

I ain't playin, Jasmine.

Then that makes two of us, Sheriff.

Reynolds shoots a suspicious, sharp look to Will:

Do you know where Katie's at?

As Will eyes him, Jasmine eyes Will until he finally shrugs:
Katie who?

Reynolds' thick features seem to accept that, and he slowly backs the cruiser up the road.

Jasmine watches after him and then comments:

That man was born stupid, and he's been losin ground ever since.

Will, starting to sense a storm of cross-currents and secrets, turns back to Jasmine:

If Katie's a suspect, why doesn't he just arrest her?

Oh he'd like ta do more than arrest her, honey. Man's married 20 years, but from the first he seen Katie, he's been chasin after her like some young-buck bachelor.

Will has to shake his head, amazed by it all:

So what exactly did he mean the other night when he said he wanted to talk to you for old time's sake?

Jasmine gives him a look:

For a boy who talks so big on cuttin line, Willy, ya sure don't let go of much. Do ya?

She walks back to the Rambler, ending their date on a terse, unsettling note, shocking Will back to the reality of life everywhere even if, for a long, hot mysterious afternoon, he had imagined it might be different down here.

Crowded into Hollister's office, three southern businessmen in suits are conferring together, with one of them warning:

Some of the boys are gettin a little concerned bout the slow progress of our mutual business interests, Mayor.

Hollister shrugs:

Good things take time, gentlemen.

Another suit leans forward:

Question is, Clarence, how much time?

Another suit adds:

And we have been patient. But the Pinch is the only thing left standin between us and our plans. Now, as you know, if the tax man should get a hold of it first, all our geological studies could end up in the public domain, which means everythin we've been workin towards the last 15 years could end up in the mud.

Hollister gives them all a testy look:

As if I don't know that? Where's your faith? I brought us all this far, didn't I?

The first suit replies for the group:

It's just that time is of the essence now, Clarence.

Another adds:

All we wanna know, Clarence, is when will the Pinch be ours so we can start drillin?

Hollister shakes his head, scolding their impatience:

Soon. All right? One way or another.

A sudden knock on the conference room door buttons everybody's lips, and Hollister calls:

Come in.

Reynolds enters and then sees the businessmen seated around the conference table:

If you're busy, Mr. Mayor, I can—

We got nothin ta hide here, Sheriff. Come on in . . . Sheriff Reynolds been investigatin the recent spate of murders in our community . . . so, any progress ta report, Sheriff?

Well that's just it, Mayor. There don't seem to be any witnesses and—

Is that what ya come all this way ta tell me? That ya got a whole lotta nothing to show for it?

As the Businessmen snicker at Reynolds' expense, Hollister adds:

Why heck, Sheriff, I could hire me a dog and end up with nothin just the same.

Reynolds adjusts his belt:

As you're well aware, Mayor, it's an ongoin investigation.

Then get on with it. Find me a killer, or I may just have ta show ya the door.

Reynolds nods and exits, after which Hollister looks back at the room:

Like I said, gentlemen: soon. One way or another.

Sunday morning arrives and finds Will still in bed, with a laptop and a still unwritten true crime novel on the desk beside it, and an envelope with yet-to-be-signed divorce documents resting expectantly on his dresser.

As he lies there, he tries to reconstruct his yesterday, and the look Jasmine gave him when he suggested selling the Pinch, not to mention the reason she gave him for not selling it.

Hours pass, and before he could account for where the minutes had escaped to, afternoon was already bending towards evening.

For her part, Jasmine spent the day beginning and abandoning little cleaning projects, designed to take her mind off things. But even a few beers could not slow her brain, so she tries to relax in a hot bath.

As she lays her head back, she hears someone moving around on her porch...

Who's there?

Will calls back as cheerfully as he can:

Is this story night?

I'm in the bath, Willy!

I can wait.

As she scowls, unable to relax in peace, he begins to pace restlessly. He then walks around to the side porch, just outside her bathroom window.

Now how'm I s'posed to relax with you struttin around out there, Willy?

Relax. I'll do the talking. 'Fact, I'll tell you a story. Well, not a story exactly. More like a...I don't know. Anyway, you ever see those crabs down by the dock?

No, Willy, I was only born here. Now what about 'em?

They have this one really big claw, and this one really tiny one, see, and while I was watching them this morning, I see one of them crawl out of his hole and start circling this other crab-guy And because he has this one huge claw, he looks like he's saying, Hey, pal, I can take you with one hand tied behind my back. That's right, pincer-face; I can take your crusty ass with just the one claw!

Jasmine hears scuffling. So she climbs from her bath and moves to the window to have a look, and sees Will acting the various parts like a little boy:

So then this crab takes his one big claw and bops this guy. Just hauls off and smacks his brother crab for no apparent reason. 'Take that!' Then he turns around and runs right back in his hole. Now, the guy who just got smacked, he's pissed, but he can't get to guy who just hit him, so he goes and smacks some poor guy who's minding his own business!

Jasmine can't help smiling, finding herself starting to fall for Will, even if she's still doing her best to resist that familiar undertow pulling at her heart.

Then the new smackee goes looking for somebody he can smack. And on and on and on. And it occurred to me: this is what we must look like from Heaven. A whole swamp to ourselves, but what do we do? We spend the little time we have going out of our way to smack each other around.

Will stops playing out the parts, still unaware he's being watched:

Real profound. I know. But we have such stories for why we do what we do. Alibis, really. This job's a good one, that one's a bad one. This marriage will last, that one won't. Alibis to explain who and what we are. A few of them may even be a little true, but most of them are just stories we tell ourselves to explain why we aren't doing what we know, deep down, we should be doing. Or could be doing, if we weren't so...afraid. But then the tide rolls in and washes all our alibis away. And then it's just us, looking up at the sky, and wondering where all the time went.

Will stares off, lost in his own thoughts as Jasmine, backing slowly away from her window, sits on the edge of her tub, moved, affected by Will.

Minutes later, Jasmine opens her door and Will enters to find her wrapped in a silk robe, her hair twisted up in a towel, her eyes appraising Will as he goes on to explain:

What I said about me leaving my wife? She was having an affair. So I guess that qualifies as why she left me.

Jasmine thinks about it before responding:

There're a lot of ways ta leave someone, Willy. And if ya do it right, you can play the executioner and the victim all at the same time.

Will waits for more, sensing a truth he can't yet articulate, as Jasmine adds:

In which case, her 'affair' may have been quite a relief.

Will turns, taken aback:

A relief? To find out your wife just spent the past year with her heels in the air? That's not a relief, Jasmine. That's a—

Will suddenly stops, faltering, registering an unexpected rush of emotions.

...a shock. A heart-wrenching, horrible...shock.

Jasmine eyes him, unconvinced:

Ya sure? Cause if I didn't know better, honey, I'd say it sounds an awful lot like one of them alibis-of-the-heart of yours.

Will raises another point:

You weren't there, Jasmine. Okay? So you don't know.

But you were there, Willy. So tell me, did ya love her pretty smile? Or the way she looked that night ya first kissed her, first won her?

As Will fills with confusion, Jasmine presses him:

Or could it be that, deep down, as time went by, all that faded and ya wanted it over, but ya just didn't want the blood on your hands?

Will shakes his head, dismissing Jasmine's narrative:

She had the affair. Not me. That was her choice, not mine.

Jasmine gently shrugs off his objection and continues:

So what was your weapon of choice, Willy? A slow, cool disinterest? All empty smiles and distracted kisses? Or did ya accuse her of just not understandin the real you?

Willy sobers, the expression on his face admitting that he did accuse Brenda of that...

I'll bet by the time you were through, Willy, no one – not even you – could pin that little murder on you. ·

Will sobers, affected.

He then starts to pace, growing agitated, wanting to deny everything, to prove how wrong she is – except that emotions, once revealed for their truth, can only be understood in the light of that truth, however inconvenient or exasperating or shattering their truth may be.

And slowly Will stops pacing and sits back down, discovering he may not be the victim, but rather the cause.

As he absorbs that, he has to smile, and as he does he turns to test Jasmine:

And what's Wheeler your alibi for?

Jasmine stiffens, no better than Will at having the tables turned:

Wheeler ain't no alibi.

You sure? Cause if I didn't know better, I'd say you've been using Wheeler as an excuse to avoid a real relationship.

With who?

With me. Or would a real relationship ruin the carefully-crafted alibi you call a life?

Jasmine stares at Will as if she can't imagine how to respond.

So Will moves to her, takes her in his arms and kisses her.

How about giving us a try?

Will kisses her again, beginning to shower her mouth, neck and breasts until Jasmine suddenly pushes him off her, confusing Will:

What?

Jasmine's eyes tangle as she pulls her bathrobe closed:

Try? Is that what you just said?

Yes. As in try a real relationship with me.

Try, Will?

What's wrong with that?

When ya say try, do ya mean like, say, when a woman tries on a new dress?

No.

Or do you mean try like when ya get an invite to a party ya don't want ta go to, but instead of just sayin no thanks, ya say you'll try ta come? Hell, Willy, if that's all ya want, I should just spread my legs right now so you can get it over with. Gee, offer like that, how could a girl refuse?

Will looks at her, shocked and exasperated:

I didn't mean it that way and you know it.

I know exactly how ya meant it, Willy. Sad part is you don't. Now get.

Excuse me?

You heard me. Get!

You gotta be kidding me.

Do I look like I'm kiddin ya, Willy?

Stunned, incredulous, Will gets up and moves to her door. But then stops and turns:

What the hell just happened here?

Jasmine's eyes fill with untold worlds of hurt and bitter betrayal:

I don't need to be tried by anyone or anything again in my life, Willy! So if that's all ya got ta offer, you can go try somebody else.

As Will steps out onto her porch, reeling, Jasmine shuts her door behind him. And Will's incredulity shifts into anger. And he turns and talks back to the door:

This from a woman who apparently can't make love to a man if she isn't dead drunk. And then it's to some dirt bag you think is somebody else. It's pathetic, Jasmine!

Will waits, but only silence answers. So he snorts and turns to go, only to then hear her door swing back open:

What's pathetic is promisin what you can't deliver, Willy!

He turns to confront her, eager to argue:

How would you know what I can or can't deliver? You're too busy being Okefenokee's resident prick tease!

Will stalks off, enraged and hurt.

Jasmine watches him a moment, shaking with anger and anguish.

A day or two pass.

As another afternoon leans into Okefenokee, Will, looking the worse for wear, walks up to the civil servant lady, who acts like she's never seen Will before:

May I help ya?

Vital Records room.

Sorry. But it's closed.

Closed?

For remodelin.

You can't be serious.

Grand reopenin be some time next year. Or the year after. All depends.

On what?

So many things, really.

She eyes him, relishing her little tyrant moment, causing Will's blood to boil:

Those are public records in there, ma'am. And if I have to—

She interrupts:

Sorry, but like I said. You'll just have ta wait for our grand reopenin.

As she gets back to her nails, Will, livid but helpless, strides back out.

When he leaves the library, he crosses the town-square park with its requisite cannon, and it gives him an idea.

So he turns back and heads right back into the library.

He marches right past the civil servant lady, and right into the main library, where he descends on the newspaper and microfiche records.

As the lady now looks on, helpless to stop Will, he rifles through records of old newspaper clippings through the rest of the afternoon, finally striking upon a photo of Jasmine, captioned 'Ananstasia Jasmine Mae Bell, widow and suspect.'

Astonished, Will reads the article, visualizing as he does...

A white man, Cassius, Jasmine's murdered ex husband, drunk, is staggering home in the dark, only to be shoved from behind.

He falls forward, just like Mason, face down into mud. As he struggles to get up, a muddy boot steps onto the back of his neck, ensuring he drowns on its silt...

Later, Will imagines Cassius' corpse being dragged from the mud while Sheriff Reynolds looks on, shaking his head...

As the article continues, Will imagines Sheriff Reynolds handcuffing Jasmine at her cottage and taking her into custody...

How say ya to the charges?

Will, shocked back into the present, whips to see Dewey, smiling, noting the article Will's reading on the microfiche monitor:

Something else, huh? Like I said, if it's crime you're interested in, Jasmine's your girl.

All it says here is she was a suspect.

That she was, for a time. So the only question is, what do ya 'suspect', Mr. Woods?

Intrigued, Will turns to Dewey for help.

Got a minute?

A minute later, as Will and Dewey stroll through the leaf-strewn park, Dewey asks:

So how's your whodunit novel comin so far?

Will shakes his head in the negative and then looks back to Dewey:

So who do you think killed Jasmine's ex?

Dewey shrugs, hazarding a guess:

Cassius? Somethin them newspaper stories failed ta mention was that Cassius also just happened to be the son of our very own Mayor.

Will stops in his tracks:

Cassius Bell was Hollister's son?

Bastard son. And not a month after they found Cassius face down by the swamp, the Mayor's city council reassessed the taxes on Jasmine's Pinch so high she couldn't afford ta keep her own inheritance.

Will's face fills with a conclusion:

In other words, you think it was Hollister.

Me? I don't know what to think, Mr. Woods. But there's no shortage of suspects down here, which while dysfunctional as ya please, is just the way we like it.

Will's had enough of this town's self-congratulatory ways:

So sheltering a murderer is the way you like it?

Dewey eyes Will, a little disappointed and then explains:

Here's what I do know, Mr. Woods: Jasmine is one of the most honest, forthright people I—

Will balks:

Honest? Forthright? Please. Let me tell you a little something about Jasmine, my friend: she's a hypocritical tease who wouldn't know a straight answer if it bit her in the ass!

Which is something I imagine you'd like ta do, Mr. Woods. That is, if I'm not mistaken?

Will's forced to uncomfortably retrench:

Look, right now, what I want is answers.

Dewey eyes Will for a moment, reading Will like a book:

We all want somethin. But the answers you want gonna depend on what ya want, and how deep ya wanna go with Jasmine: a few inches up her vagina, or all the way deep into her heart. Choice is yours, Mr. Woods.

Dewey gives Will a look and then heads on his way, leaving Will to watch after him, reeling.

That night, Jasmine drives up to find Will sitting on her porch again.

She climbs impassively from the Rambler and walks to her door. On her way, she observes:

Make yourself at home; why don't ya?
Went to the library today.
Jasmine hesitates, ready to close her door:
Found my true crime story. And the kicker is: it's you.
Ya don't say.
Jasmine shuts her door.
So Will continues, talking though her closed door:
*So in the interests of fairness, I'd like to hear your side of
the story. Course, if you won't talk to me, then all I have to go on
is what other people say about you.*

A quiet beat. Then Jasmine opens her door. Will thinks he's
hooked her. But instead:
Where's your phone?
My phone?
It records stuff, right? Give it to me.
He digs in his pocket and hands her his phone.
*Only reason I'm doin this, Willy, is cause I, for one, finish
what I start.*
She slips it into her pocket, and closes her door again.
Will waits, incredulous. Then he talks to her door again:
*Let me get this straight: you'll tell me your side of the story
to my phone, but not to my face?*
Her silence on the other side of the door answers the
question, and Will's finally reduced to giving up and going back
to his cottage to await her recording.

Back in town, Reynolds steps back into his Sheriff's office,
tired from his day, to be startled when he sees Katie waiting for
him, looking scared and nervous.
Reynolds moves to his desk, trying to control his own
sudden case of nerves.
So where ya been, Katie?
To hell and back. How bout you?
Their eyes lock – an unfinished history between them:
Would ya like a cup of—
Let's just get this over with, shall we, Sheriff?
Reynolds adjusts and dutifully continues:
So what can ya tell me bout Mason's murder?
Nothin.

Reynolds considers it, containing himself:

So you don't know—

Nothin bout nothin. That's right.

Katie's eyes are now glaring into his as Reynolds looks up, only half-sarcastic when he asks:

So what do ya know, Katie?

She smiles warily:

I know if I go to church long enough and hard enough, one day, by God's grace, I just might feel genuinely sorry for what happened ta Mason. And when that day comes, then I'll know I'll be truly through with him – through his beatings, through with his humiliations, through with his memory – once and for all. Now are we done?

Reynolds seems to get lost in himself for a moment, so Katie stands and starts to leave when she hears him resuming:

If they put either one of ya on trial for the murders, and fail ta convict, they won't ever be able to try ya again.

Katie shakes her head, filled with sarcasm:

My, are you comfortin?

Can I come see ya?

My bed's for men who defend me. Not accuse me, Sheriff.

With that, Katie walks out as Reynolds clouds over, stung.

Will is seated at his laptop computer in his cottage, trying to get his novel started; but he hears a car engine, so he gets up and peers out his window to see…a police cruiser pulling up, creeping to a stop outside Jasmine's cottage.

A moment later, Reynolds climbs out, pushing his world-weary frame to Jasmine's door.

He knocks and waits.

Soon Jasmine opens it. She takes one look at Reynolds and gushes:

That's right, I killed him, Sheriff. I killed Mason, just like I done killed Cassius before him.

She holds out her wrists as if to welcome his handcuffs, but Reynolds just stares at her. So she demands:

What, ya think I ain't capable of such a heinous act?

To protect Katie? In a heart beat.

Well don't that just make us two peas in a pod.

Reynolds darkens over:

Mark my words, Jasmine: one way or another, I'm gonna get ta the bottom of this.

Whose bottom, Sheriff?

My bottom.

Careful. Ya might just get your head stuck up your own bottom.

Jasmine shuts her door in Reynolds' face.

Reynolds stands there a beat, brooding.

His eyes then travel to Will's cottage, and Will, spying on him, dodges away from his window to avoid being seen.

Will waits, crouching down, wondering if he's been discovered.

But then he hears the police cruiser start back up and creep away, its tires crunching the leaves before fading into the buzz of the crickets.

Galvanizing into action, Will moves to his laptop and sets to work, eager to start getting this all down.

Early the next morning, as gray skies hover over Okefenokee, bringing with them a heavy, sticky humidity, Will is still at his laptop, notating various articles on the murders, assembling the pieces of his novel.

After a mid morning nap, he grabs his bag and heads back to the library for more, irritating the civil servant lady no end.

By afternoon, with sunshine breaking through to warm things up and brighten the skies, Will returns home with an armload of photocopies to find his cellphone behind by his screen door, placed there by Jasmine.

He looks around, but Jasmine's cottage is quiet, so he picks it up, exasperated by her methods, and heads into his cottage.

As he settles in for another evening's manic work at his laptop, he finds his eyes traveling to his phone...

Finally giving in to his curiosity, he picks his cellphone and, navigating to the play function, listens to Jasmine's sultry voice effortlessly taking him to those far off days to see...

As Gabe buries the bottle of moonshine, stashing it for his rendezvous with Chastity, a shadow of a man crawls over his back...

Gabe spins around to see Orlando, drunk, raising a leather belt to whip Gabe. But instead of running, Gabe just stands there, defying his father.

Incensed, Orlando lashes Gabe:

You little thief!

Orlando lashes Gabe again. But Gabe takes it, locked-jawed, as Megan runs from the house, desperate, yelling at Orlando to stop.

But Orlando just begins to strike Megan too.

Gabe instantly maneuvers himself between his father and mother, absorbing the lashes meant for his mother, until Orlando's fury ebbs, and he sobers into a soul-crushing shame.

Horrified, Orlando retrieves the stolen bottle of moonshine from Gabe and retreats back into the Tool Shed as Gabe and Megan look on, trembling with rage, sadness and desperation.

Later, as Megan tries to treat Gabe's wounds, Gabe looks on stoically.

He didn't mean it, Gabe. It's just he's sick.

What if I wasn't here and he came for you, ma? What then?

Gabe gets up and goes outside, wondering how he'll ever be able to protect his mother...until he senses another presence.

Gabe suddenly turns to see Crebbs emerging from the shadows with a twisted grin:

Hello, boy.

What do ya want?

Where's your daddy at, boy?

Gabe just stares at Crebbs, on the verge of telling him, but then lies:

I don't know.

Crebbs considers it and then counters:

Chastity likes ya. A whole lot. Ain't never seen her like this before.

How do you—?

There ain't much I don't know, Gabe.

Gabe's face drains as Crebbs looks right through him, until Crebbs forces a smile to admit:

Except where your daddy's at. But no matter. Sure enough I'll find him, sooner or later. And when I do I'm gonna have a talk with him concernin that temper of his.

Tears start to boil up from Gabe's eyes:

I ain't no whippin post.

And that's exactly what I'm gonna tell him, soon as ya tell me where he's at. In the meantime, I'm sure Chastity be glad ta lick your wounds, if ya like...?

A thousand more emotions storm through Gabe's tortured heart, and he hears himself say:

He...might be in the tool shed.

Crebbs offers a slow, rotten-toothed smirk as Gabe aches with a sudden guilt:

That a boy. Now you go on now. Chastity's waitin for ya. I guarantee it.

As Gabe moves out into the dark night, he hears a crane cry out over the shadowy swamp.

A moment later, Chastity walks into view from the tall grasses, her hair a thicket of knots.

She stares at Gabe, unnerving him.

She then lies down, submissive, but looks away as if prepared to dutifully endure his affections.

Gabe's heart pounds. He lies down beside her. Then he slowly tries to touch her. But she suddenly recoils, which frightens Gabe, so he tries to talk to her:

How do you know Crebbs?

Chastity looks at Gabe strangely, like he should know:

Crebbs is my daddy.

As Gabe is filled with horror, Crebbs is eyeing an ashen-faced Orlando as they sit down with a collection of card sharks around a poker table in town:

This here's Orlando, Gentlemen. He's nobody's fool, so ya better watch yourselves, and your wallets!

Crebbs gestures for a waiter to bring Orlando a drink as a dealer fans out a deck of cards for Orlando to cut.

Orlando cuts the cards, and the dealer carries on, tossing out the cards around the table to the men who, long accustomed to skinning fools, keep their cards, and their intentions, close to their chests.

As the long night wears on, the sharks skin Orlando hand by hand, distracting him along the way by cajoling, encouraging and flattering him, covering their cheating and misdeeds by tactically allowing him the occasional win, only to clean him out on the next, drawing him further and further into debt until he feels like a man sinking in quicksand pit, desperate to make any bargain that will free him from its pull.

For their part, the card sharks shake their heads, feigning sympathy for his losing streak while Crebbs, motioning a server to bring Orlando another drink, settles in for the kill.

He lost till there was nothin left to lose. In a few hours, they'd taken everythin he'd ever worked for: his money, his belongins, and most of all, they took the deed to his land. At least they thought they had. And when they were through, they tossed him out inta the street, without so much as a ride home.

Will imagines Orlando staggering, his anguished eyes streaming with stinging tears.

Arriving back at his cabin, he weeps, sure now that it is lost to him forever…

So even though he could face down a 'gator, he couldn't face his family. Not after what he'd done. Not even if they still woulda taken him back. Which they would have. If he'd only let 'em.

Tormented, Orlando turns back to the tool shed, his face darkening with a new thought...

Walking home from his bleak rendezvous with Chastity, Gabe suddenly sees Jojo running down the road, desperately trying to get away from something.

The instant she sees Gabe, he beckons to her to follow him into the swamp.

But just as they escape into the wilds, a gunshot blast rings out in the night – just as the recording abruptly comes to an end.

Will, dreaming at his desk, is startled back to the present. *What the hell?*

Gathering his wits, he checks his cell phone to discover Jasmine has filled its memory full – exceeded its capacity to record her tale.

Will leans back, feeling fevered, as if he has just awakened from a vivid nightmare.

The next morning, he walks back into the diner to find the coffee counter full. So he moves past it, to the last available booth in back.

Jasmine, serving a plate of scrambled eggs and gravy-smothered biscuits, notes his arrival, inwardly preparing for the meeting when she moves to his back booth:

Ya orderin somethin ta eat?

Why are you telling me this story?

Because ya asked. Now what'll it be?

Is it true?

She considers, then:

True as me and true as you.

In other words: you're not going to tell me why you're telling me this gruesome little tale, are you?

Like I said: I finish what I—

Start. I know. Well allow me to finish what never started, and that is some free, professional advice. Sell the Pinch to Hollister. Now. While you still can.

Jasmine considers simply walking away, but then digs in:

Ya already gave me that advice, Willy, despite the fact that I never asked for it.

Will shakes his head, dumbfounded.

Why ya care, Willy? Ain't your problem.

Look: the government's just going to turn around and auction it off to the highest bidder. Which means Hollister's going to get it, anyway. And at pennies on the dollar. But if you sell it to him now, you might even turn a profit. So what I'm advising you in the strongest, possible terms, Jasmine, is to cut line while you still have a line to cut!

She eyes him, turning steely:

If you're not orderin something ta eat, I'm afraid I'm gonna have ta ask ya ta leave.

Will shakes his head, disgusted:

Know what your problem is down here? It's all the self-mythologizing, self-romanticizing bullshit you people habitually substitute for rational thinking or real feelings. Not to mention your artery-clogging nostalgia for some long-lost golden age that never existed in the first place! Or if it did, it was only for the rich and the few! You spend your lives pining away for a fantasy you yourselves invented, just so you wouldn't have to deal with things the way they are.

Will gets up to go:

Well as far as I'm concerned, you can have it, and you keep it!

Jasmine stands her ground:

No doubt you're right, Will. Who else would know more about creatin fantasies to avoid dealin with hisself?

Really. And how do you figure that?

Down here, we call our fantasy Dixie. You, on the other hand, Willy, call yours "Brenda".

Will stares at her, stung, but then manages to counter with:

No, Jasmine, you call yours Wheeler. And you're going to keep on calling Wheeler because he's exactly what you deserve!

With that, Will strides out of the diner.

Jasmine watches after him, stung and shaken. But when her customers start calling for more coffee, she pulls herself back together and gets back to work.

Over at Bubba's bar, only just open for the day, Clarence Hollister, alone, lost in thought, nurses a drink as the young bartender sets up for the day.

Did you know that your average male 'gator, if given a chance, will eat his young?

The bartender winces at the thought as he works, which only seems to encourage Hollister to muse:

I'd even go so far ta venture he considers it a culinary delicacy. An acquired taste, perhaps, eatin one's offspring. But to the 'gator, a most desirable, delectable and tender morsel.

Hollister looks at the Bartender to see his reaction.

The bartender makes a queasy face, hoping to quiet Hollister. But Hollister grins and replies:

So it's up to the momma' 'gator ta defend her pups against they own papa. Because if she don't, he's gonna show them how things really are in this world of ours, even if he's gotta eat 'em ta teach 'em. – But then, better ta die knowin the truth, than ta live under the delusion of a lie. Wouldn't ya say?

The Bartender tries to change the subject:

Feels like another scorcher today.

Hollister continues, undaunted:

Yes, suh, the 'gator's been around for millions of years. Know why? Cause he knows the real secret of life. Now, it's not the kinda thing ya liable ta hear in Sunday school. But it's the secret that's insured his legacy to this very day.

The bartender tries to look busy, but Hollister's not to be ignored:

Don't ya wanna know the gator's secret?

The Bartender reluctantly obliges by stopping to listen:

What gator learned ta do many millennia ago was ta take whatever he wanted, whenever he wanted and however he wanted it. And he don't let nothin get in his way. So if it's a snack he wants, and one of his pups happens by, he don't waste no time hesitatin. He just…

Hollister bites at the air, imitating an alligator biting into its own pup.

As the bartender gets back to work, Hollister looks around, then:

Ya right. Gonna be another scorcher.

Back at the cottages, the day tiptoes into the evening and then slips away into the night as Will sits at his desk typing away on his laptop, filling up a first chapter of a whodunit unfolding under his fingers, and outside his door.

However, as Will types, lost in his work, a large shadow suddenly fills up his screen door:

Mr. Woods?

Will starts and turns around to see Sheriff Reynolds' lumbering silhouette at his door. But he then needs a beat to ride out the adrenaline rush coursing through his veins:

Didn't mean ta startle ya, Mr. Woods.

What is it, Sheriff?

66

Got a moment?

Will moves to open his screen door and Reynolds steps in.

They nod awkwardly. Reynolds gestures to a chair, and Will invites him to take a seat.

Seated across from each other, Reynolds seems uncharacteristically thoughtful, reflective, even uncertain about something and he suddenly comments:

I just can't believe that today is Tuesday.

Will waits for more:

I take it ya heard about the recent murders which have so ravaged this little community of ours?

What about them?

How'd ya hear?

Excuse me?

Who told ya about the murders?

Jasmine.

And what, exactly, did she say about 'em?

She said something about there being a couple of recent murders that ravaged this little community.

As Reynolds stiffens at Will's uncooperative attitude, Will tries to turn the tables:

Mind if I ask you a question? Other than Jasmine and Katie, were there ever any other suspects?

I don't see where that's any of your business, Mr. Woods.

I'm just trying to give you a chance to tell your side of the story.

My side? Ya act like it's me who's on trial here.

Nobody's on trial here, Sheriff. And that's my point, because nobody's ever been on trial, for either murder.

Reynolds' thick features turn opaque:

Your real point, Mr. Woods, should be that ya don't know squat. Ya just think ya do.

So enlighten me.

How?

Well, for starters, did Cassius and/or Mason have any enemies?

Does a duck poop?

So give me a for-instance?

How about the fact that Cassius beat Dewey up so bad one time that he ended up in a hospital.

Dewey? Why Dewey?

On account of Dewey's sexual persuasion.

So was he charged?

Oh I arrested Cassius sure enough, but nothing came of it.

Why not?

Cause Dewey refused ta press charges. Just like Jasmine and Katie. They just always refused ta press charges.

I heard Mason beat Katie up, but are you telling me Cassius beat Jasmine up?

Reynolds looks flatly at Will and then replies:

He was what ya might call a mean drunk. So whether he meant to or not, that's what he did, and more than once.

You think they had something to do with their murders? Or do you think it was Dewey?

Reynolds climbs to his feet, noting Will's laptop:

Writin a book about it all, are ya?

Trying to. Which is why I'd appreciate anything you can tell me.

Solvin a murder takes evidence, Mr. Woods. You're just makin up a story. There's a difference.

Is there? I'm not so sure there always is, Sheriff. And I was a lawyer.

Was a lawyer?

Why do I get the feeling you know who the murderer is, or at least you think you do?

Reynolds considers it and smiles.

I'll bet you were a good lawyer, Mr. Woods. Ya have a pleasant evenin now.

With that, Reynolds nods and leaves, leaving Will with more burning questions that before his visit.

The next morning, Will surprises Dewey by arriving early to his office.

Dewey looks up from his desk cheerfully:

Why Mr. Woods, aren't you bright and early? What can I do for you?

Can I take a moment of your time?

Certainly. Have a seat. Is it about the cottage?
No. It's about Jasmine's ex. Cassius.
Dewey quickly sobers.
What about him, Mr. Woods?

A few minutes later, as Will looks on, Dewey leans back in his office chair:
Why didn't she press charges?
Will explains:
He beat her, didn't he?
Dewey considers:
I really don't think I should be speakin for Jasmine on this matter.
But why'd she marry a guy like Cassius in the first place?
Your judgment is always perfect when it comes to people, is it, Mr. Woods?
As Will shrugs, conceding the point, Dewey looks outside.
Walk and talk?

Minutes later, Will and Dewey take another stroll in the small, nearby park, offering Will an opening to ask his real question:
So why didn't you press charges?
Dewey stops, caught off-guard. He eyes Will a beat and then asks:
Been doin your research, have ya?
So?
Dewey is silent a moment and then sighs cryptically:
If I had, Cassius' good-ol'-boy pals woulda formed a line halfway round the block, just waitin ta take their turns where Cassius left off.
So what did you do?
An iron-willed look fills Dewey's face:
What did I do? I lay there in that bed till I could walk. Then I got up, and I walked home.
And then?
And then one Cassius Blessington met his maker.
Dewey walks on. Will watches after him, almost certain he's found his killer.

As Will arrives back, he finds a cassette recorder by his door.

He picks it up to find a cassette inside and then looks over at Jasmine's cottage.

You gotta be kidding me.

Entering his cottage, Will tosses the cassette aside and goes to the sink to pat some cool water on his face. But as he does, he finds himself eyeing the recorder.

Annoyed that he can't resist, he retrieves the recorder and presses play, once more falling prey to Jasmine's sordid tale, once more envisioning Crebbs striding out onto the Pinch, looking around like a kid counting his birthday presents.

He locates Megan as she pumps water from a well and hands her an I.O.U., signed by Orlando the night before at the card game.

Sorry ta bother ya at such a time, but business is business. And ya are on my land, after all.

Megan takes the I.O.U., looks it over and hands it back to Crebbs.

And I'm sorry ta inform ya, Mr. Crebbs, but my husband was gamblin with chips that weren't his ta gamble.

Crebbs' eyes narrow:

What are ya talkin bout?

I'm sayin this here land belongs ta...Gabe. You can check the deed down at the county records if ya like. But far as your winnin's is concerned, ya ain't got none. But then, ya wasn't the only fella that got taken that night, was ya?

Crebbs eyes her for a long beat and then says:

One way or another, Ms. Megan, I'm gonna collect what's owed me. One way or the other.

Crebbs tips his hat, his eyes full of menace, as he hobbles off... Jasmine's recorded story continues:

And from that day forward, Crebbs had it in his heart ta get that land. Not because he needed it. But because Crebbs believed the innocent in the world ought to be punished.

Crebbs suddenly stops in his tracks, reverses pivot, and then looks back at Megan with a violent lust in his eyes. He then starts back towards the cabin, hell-bent to collect something for his troubles.

Megan sees him headed back her way, and tries to run inside the cabin for protection just as, down by the swamp, Gabe is returning home.

As he rounds a bend, he sees an orange glow lighting the sky over the treetops, located in the direction of what would be his home.

Alarmed, Gabe takes off running, only to arrive back home to find his cabin home ablaze.

He shouts, calling for his mother. But when Megan doesn't answer, he braves the flames to enter the cabin and billowing black smoke to find her unconscious on the floor, right where Crebbs left her.

Scooping her up into his arms, he carries her out to safety.

Everythin woulda burned ta the ground, except that was the night that Orlando's tears finally fell. All the tears he could never shed in this life fell from heavens that night. And there were so many of 'em that they put that fire out.

A sudden cloudburst results in a hard downpour that quickly extinguishes the flames, leaving a smoking, half-burned cabin in its wake as Gabe looks around...and the cassette clicks off.

Will is startled back to the present, and quickly flips the cassette, eager to hear more. Bu the flip side is blank.

That's it? Oh come on, damn it!

Moments later, Will bangs on Jasmine's cottage door.

No answer comes, so he bangs harder.:

Willy?

Then what happened?

Jasmine cracks her door:

Then what?

Will shoves the cassette at her:

Finish what you started.

She eyes the cassette, then him, and then slowly opens her door, allowing him to enter.

A minute later, back at her kitchen table, he listens as she continues, clutching her robe close as she relates:

Megan died givin birth to Crebbs' seed. But since Orlando had signed the deed over ta Gabe, Crebbs couldn't claim the land. So it stayed with Gabe.

Will waits for more, but Jasmine's gone quiet.

Wait, that's it? That's the end?

What'd you expect, Willy, a bed of roses?

No. But I expected an ending.

In that case, Willy, maybe you best write one. See if you can make it come out nice, too, cause I can't.

What do you mean?

I mean finish what ya started, for once in your life.

Will looks at her, incredulous, then bemused, then incensed – but realizing she really does mean to end her story there:

Fine. Whatever. But that isn't the end and you know it.

My, my Willy, you do go on.

Will's face fills with disgust, and he's about to say something, but then just throws up his hands and walks out.

As he crosses back to his cottage, he shakes his head, running an inner dialogue about cutting line, washing his hands of it all.

But as the wee hours pass, Will tosses and turns, reliving Jasmine's story in a half-conscious state…

In his dream, he finds himself out in the swamp alone, just like Gabe in Jasmine's story.

It's dark and eerie and as he makes his way through the overgrowth, he arrives at a muddy bank to discover a white man's corpse, face down in the mud.

He draws near, compelled to discover who it might be, and as he reaches ever-so-gingerly down to roll it over and reveal its face, he discovers its Megan.

But before he can grieve, her eyes suddenly pop open, wild-eyed, grinning.

Will staggers back in terror and then takes off running through the swamp's backwoods, rushing through tall grasses and branches that cut at his skin, until he comes upon a small cabin with a dim light glowing in its window.

So Will veers towards it and then slows to sneak up to the window.

When he peers in, just as in the story when Gabe did the same, he sees what looks to be Crebbs at his table, eating his supper.

Will slips, making a noise.

Crebbs stops eating, and slowly, slowly turns to reveal that he's an alligator.

As Will reacts in horror, he hears something behind him and whips around to see Sheriff Reynolds, pulling his gun, aiming it at him!

So Will takes off running again, escaping, panicked, as Sheriff Reynolds chases him. Suddenly he is able to move like a Gazelle, gaining on Will.

So Will angles for the swamp waters, only to see a man on its banks, the scene looking exactly like his childhood photo, including the handkerchief hanging from the man's back pocket:

Help! Help me!

The man slowly turns as Will arrives to discover that the man is Hollister.

Will pulls up short, stunned as Hollister's grins becomes a mocking laugh, echoing out into the swamp, scattering the cranes and calling the alligators to swarm…Then Will is suddenly shocked back awake, to fall from his bed onto the floor.

He lies there for a moment in panicked revelation, breathing hard.

Moments later, he scrambles to his feet and charges out.

In a frenzy, he pounds on Jasmine's cottage door again:
Jasmine!

Yanked from her sleep, Jasmine finally opens it, alarmed:
What you want now, Willy? What is it?

You're Gabe! And Katie's Jojo. You switched all the boys for girls in the story, didn't you? Which means Chastity's…Cassius! But then you switched it back because Crebbs has got to be Hollister? That's it, isn't it?

Jasmine's face turns opaque as Will insists:

That's why you've been telling me this story, isn't it …Well, isn't it?

As Will's eyes burn at Jasmine, she seems to grow more cool and collected:

Looks like Willy-boy done got hisself a real whodunit story.

But if Chastity's actually Cassius, why did Gabe – I mean you – marry her – I mean him? Why'd you marry Cassius?

…Ta make amends.

Will's face crinkles with confusion:

For what?

Stop thinkin like a lawyer for once, Willy, and start thinkin like a man.

Jesus, Jasmine. Just tell me why. Okay? Straight out.

I married him ta make amends for what I done to my daddy. As a penance. Or can't ya understand that?

Will's staring at her, incredulous.

It's okay, Willy, took me a long time ta understand it, too.

So what am I to believe, Jasmine?

Believe what you want, honey. Most folks do anyway.

The night finds Will pacing again, beside himself.

As he does, he hears Jasmine's Rambler start up outside, and he dashes out to confront her.

As she tries to drive away, he pounds on her window until she stops and rolls it down:

So who done it, Jasmine? Who killed Cassius? Who killed Mason? Was it the same person, or a bunch of you all at once?

Jasmine just eyes him, declining to speak:

Or was it Dewey? It was Dewey, right? For revenge?

Jasmine has to smile:

Dewey?

He's the only other person I know who had the motive, the opportunity—

It wasn't Dewey, honey. Trust me.

With that, Jasmine accelerates away, forcing Will to let go of her car door. But as he watches her drive off, his blood boils:

Oh no, you don't!

Will runs to his Chevy, hops in, fires it up and speeds off after her.

Jasmine pulls into the Pinch, continues down its winding road and parks. Will, in pursuit, pulls in after her and bumps down the narrow road to pull up behind her Rambler.

He then jumps from the Chevy and runs after her, catching up:

Leave me alone, Willy.

Then it was Wheeler! You and Katie put him up to it! He'd do anything you tell him. And that's why you have to keep sleeping with him, so he'll keep his big mouth shut. That's it, isn't it?

You're overestimatin me, honey. And underestimatin Wheeler.

You said yourself he'd be around when everybody else went away!

Jasmine shoots him a sharp look:

Why is that you always have ta have another man between you and the woman you claim ya want, Willy? Why's that?

What the hell are you even talking about?

First it's your wife's affair, now Wheeler. Really, Willy. I think ya prefer it that way. Keeps ya safe from havin ta deal with a real relationship.

Will is ignited:

Me? Safe? Look who's talking!

Jasmine just shrugs as she takes out a cigarette:

Wasn't Wheeler, honey.

Then the only two is you and Katie. You helped her with her problem, and she helped you with yours!

As Jasmine smiles mysteriously, they hear a truck arriving and Will whips around to see Wheeler pulling into the Pinch.

Will snarls:

You gotta be goddamn kidding me.

Wheeler parks and climbs out, ready to fight:

Oh this night just keeps getting better and better!

Thought I told ya ta stay away from Jasmine, boy.

Listen you brain-fried cracker—

Wheeler charges at Will. They tumble to the ground, trading blows.

As they grapple, Jasmine jumps into the fray, yelling:

He's just writin about the murders, honey, okay? That's all he's here for. That's all he wants. That's all he come here for!

Will suddenly releases his grip.

Wheeler, confused, takes a moment, but then releases his, too, to see dark epiphany washing over Will's face.

Will looks over at Jasmine, like a man seeing the truth, like Paul on the road to Damascus:

...That's it, isn't it? All of it.

He climbs slowly to his feet:

All the talk, all the taking me around, showing me things, talking me up, telling me stories.

Wheeler looks worried:

What things ya been showin him, Jasmine?

It's not what ya think, darlin. And that goes for ya both.

But Will won't be denied:

No. It was all to shape what I think. So I'd end up writing your side of the story for you?

He looks around, flabbergasted, bemused:

You planned all of it, leading me on, dropping little hints, clues, just to keep my interest, tease me into thinking it was you, just so, in the end, I'd gallantly reject all that nonsense and ride to your rescue by implicating everybody but you. Then you'd have a book—an alibi in black and white – for all the world to see. Isn't that what you wanted?

Jasmine allows him his rant, not raising a finger to object or correct him as Will concludes:

You're right, Jasmine. I should've listened better!

Wheeler, still at a loss, looks to Jasmine for explanation:

What's he talkin about?

Jasmine sides with Wheeler to avoid another fisticuffs, even though her heart burns to explain it all to Will – but not in front of Wheeler:

Who knows, honey? Cause I'm sure I don't.

Will, feeling emotionally stripped bare, shakes his head:

Played me like a fiddle, Jasmine.

You wanted a true whodunit story. Well ya got what you wanted, Willy. So what do I get? Huh?

You get...him.

Will nods towards Wheeler. He then turns, walks back to the Chevy and climbs in. Jasmine watches after him as Will maneuvers the Chevy around the truck – everything in her wanting to scream at him to stay – as Will slows to give her one, last hurt look:

I really thought we...

Will gives up mid-sentence and accelerates away as Wheeler looks on, still confused:

Where's he think he's goin?

He's vanishin, honey. Can't you see that?

The next morning, the sun's up early, turning the day hot before noon. Jasmine is rocking on her porch as Katie walks up and looks around, noting the absence of Will's Chevy.

Where'd Willy go off so early?

Looks like he's gone, darlin. For good.

As Katie storms over, registering the implications, they look over to see Reynolds' cruiser pulling up the road, followed by a dusty sedan.

Sheriff Reynolds parks and climbs out:

What ya want now, Sheriff?

Katie. You're...

Reynolds falters:

What? I'm what?

Under arrest.

Katie stares at Reynolds, thunderstruck as Jasmine explodes:

For what, Sheriff?

For the murder of Mason Carver.

Lord knows you're stupid, Sheriff, but I never thought you was—

But she stops when she sees Hollister climbing from the Sedan, wearing a knowing look.

Jasmine gets the picture and looks back at Reynolds:

Shoulda figured as much.

Reynolds, chagrined, escorts a nervous Katie into his cruiser and then drives her away as Hollister advances on Jasmine:

We've had our...differences over the years, Jasmine. And I know I have my faults as a man, but let's face facts, shall we? Regardless of how ya feel bout me, it's in your own best interests ta sell me the Pinch now, while ya still can.

Jasmine leans back onto her porch chair and shakes her head, marveling at his single-mindedness and then replies:

Clarence, I wouldn't sell ya the Pinch ta save my life. Because everythin ya touch, ya make dirty.

Hollister shrugs; he's heard far worse:

Pretty high and mighty talk, especially from a girl who betrayed her own flesh and blood. Sold her own daddy down the river just ta satisfy her intemperate loins.

Jasmine doesn't bother to respond, so he continues:

Tell me somethin, Jasmine, was it worth it? Because looks ta me like ya done sold your own father for a roll in the grass and a Pinch of land that won't be yours by the end of the week.

I paid my penance, Clarence. And one day, you're gonna have ta pay yours.

Hollister dismisses her with a curled lip:

In the meantime, Katie's gonna have some pretty serious attorney fees on her back. Heavens, I wonder where she's gonna get that kind of money? But then, maybe a friend'll lend it ta her. Somebody who just came inta a little extra, say from sellin some land? Cause lord knows, ya don't want ta go to court without a good lawyer these days.

Hollister tips his hat, climbs back into the Sedan and it drives away.

Jasmine watches after him, only then allowing the tears welling up inside her to roll down her cheeks.

Meanwhile, back out on the open highway, Will speeds north, heading back to Chicago to lick his wounds.

Along the way he grumbles a blue streak as his radio pumps out Elvis' She Ain't Nuthin but a Hound dog.

If she thinks I'm going to write a whole damn book just so she can wreak revenge on a bunch of southern-fried sonofabitches, she's got another thing coming.

But the intended effect of name-calling isn't doing the trick, especially because the stinging thought at the back of his mind suddenly accosts his consciousness, and he finds himself braking hard and pulling over just to handle its resentment-shattering force.

Will sits there a moment on the side of a lonely highway, coming to terms. Finally he tells himself:

It just would be really nice, William, if just once in your life, you actually could cut line. ...Really nice.

He hangs a screeching u-turn and accelerates back the way he came, back down south, heading again for Okefenokee.

Meanwhile, back at Reynolds' office, Jasmine stoically endures Officer Hales as he fingerprints and then walks her into a holding cell, followed in by Reynolds.

Katie shakes her head:

I always thought you were a man, Sheriff. Guess I was wrong.

Humiliated, Reynolds lowers his eyes, locks her cell and then leaves.

As Will speeds along, nearing Okefenokee again, his Chevy's engine temperature gauge begins to spike, and he starts to talk to his Chevy:

Oh come on. What is your problem? ...No, come on!

A moment later, the engine begins to sputter and hiss and then billow steam, so Will reluctantly pulls over to the road's shoulder and climbs out to have a look under the hood.

As he raises it up, a blast of steam greets him, sending Will back so fast that he lands on his butt.

Later, as Will dozes into the evening in the humid heat, slumped over in his Chevy, a pair of tow truck headlights pull up behind him, followed by the dark outline of a short, wide man.

As Will comes to, he groggily looks out his window to find none other than Wheeler staring down at him.

Will reacts with a start, bracing for violence.

But Wheeler just walks back to his tow truck, climbs in and maneuvers it in front of the Chevy; then he climbs out again and starts hitching it to his truck.

He then addresses Will:

You can ride back there. Or you can ride up in the truck with me.

A minute hence, Will and Wheeler find themselves traveling down the road in an uneasy silence, until Wheeler's eyes suddenly fix on something ahead.

Wheeler suddenly brakes hard, grabs a spray paint can from under his seat and hops out.

Will watches from the truck as Wheeler sprays a circle around what looks to be a dead animal and then returns to hop back in the truck, and off they drive again.

After some more stony silence, Will can't resist from asking:

What was all that about?

Just a little somethin I come up with. Ta insure freshness.

Will waits for more, quietly horrified, as Wheeler explains:

See, I spray-paint a circle round the road-kill I find on the way in, so that on my way home, I know which one's which. Get it? That way, if it's circled, I leave it. But if it isn't, I know it's fresh, and then I got me some free, tasty eats. Hell, ya can't beat the price, now can ya?

Wills stares ahead, his worst fantasies about Wheeler confirmed, until something in Will starts to doubt himself long enough, finally making him turn back to Wheeler:

No damn way.

Wheeler's eyes sharpen as if he's offended, but then brighten as he explodes into a wild cackle, slapping at the dashboard and stomping his feet:

But I had ya goin for a minute there, didn't I, you Yankee sonofabitch!

Not really.

Admit it! I saw yo face, boy! You were hook, line and sinker, and you know it!

…Yeah, well so what? Big deal. Congratulations.

Yes siree, folks, we's gonna have us some delectable road-kill stew tonight! Mmm-mm, that is goooood!

Will takes it on the chin:

I'm glad I made your day.

*My day? I'm gonna be telling my grandkids about this day,
Bubba!*

But Wheeler suddenly catches him and sobers.

I mean...I meant...I'm sorry.

Wheeler looks positively embarrassed. Will looks over,
confused as Wheeler tries to apologize:

*I didn't mean ta refer ta me havin grandkids. On account of
your...*

My what?

Accident. Jasmine told me. Off the record, of course.

She told you what, exactly?

Wheeler looks strained:

Look, I said I'm sorry, and she made me promise.

What did she tell you, Wheeler?

About your – ya know – injury?

Wheeler tries to delicately indicate Will's groin:

Down there?

What about it?

*About the fact that you can't have kids, much less have...ya
know.*

As Wheeler hems and haws, Will finally catches on, and,
after further consideration, decides to play along. So he explodes
with mock exasperation:

*She told you? Goddamnit. I swear, you can't tell women
anything!*

Wheeler, relieved, joins in:

*Oh you said a mouthful there, Bubba! The good lord makes
'em out of our ribs, and what do they do? They turn around and
punch us in the stomach! Am I right?*

You can't trust 'em as far as you can throw them!

Oh don't even get me started, brother!

As Wheeler seems to really take to heart their unexpected
bonding, he suddenly feels the need to explain something else:

*Course that don't mean Jasmine killed Cassius. Cause she
didn't.*

How can you be so sure she didn't?

Wheeler shrugs as if it's obvious:

On account of the contract.

What contract?

Cassius himself told me there was no way he was gonna go through with it.

Go through with what?

Sell his interest in the Pinch ta his Daddy the Mayor.

Since when did Cassius have an interest in the Pinch?

Wheeler looks at Will like he's a little slow:

Ya sure you're a lawyer, Willy?

Will bites his tongue and waits for Wheeler to continue, which Wheeler finally does:

On account of his bein married ta Jasmine! But he said his daddy done spit on him his whole life, and he wasn't gonna take it no more, so we was tearin up that contract. And speakin of the devil—

They pass by Hollister, exiting a restaurant with his businessmen cronies.

As Will eyes Hollister, he sees Hollister reach into his back pocket and pull out a handkerchief – just like the one in Will's boyhood photo – spinning Will into an emotional maelstrom.

Wheeler senses the change and asks:

Ya all right?

Will, his mind racing, suddenly pulls out his cellphone and makes a call as Wheeler looks on while driving:

Jim? It's me, Will. I need you to do me a favor, okay? I'm sorry it's so late, but I need another favor from the firm's guy. ...Yes, tonight!

Later, as Wheeler deposits the Chevy at the repair shop, Will turns to him:

Mind if I bed down at your place tonight?

Wheeler, instantly uneasy, hesitates:

Why?

Cause I can't get done what needs to get done any other way.

Wheeler's still suspicious, so Will gives up.

Forget it; I'll sleep in my car.

But Wheeler objects:

No, no. It's okay. I can handle myself.

The next day, Will strolls into the diner casually and flops into a booth as if everything is just fine and dandy.

Jasmine catches sight of him, and her heart skips a few bears before she can settle it down enough to come over to him.

Well, look what that cat dragged in.

Nice to see you, too.

Can't say I expected ta see ya.

Well, I felt...guilty.

Guilty? Bout what?

About not being straight with you.

Jasmine waits for more, so Will offers:

Look, there's no easy way to say this, so I'll just come right out and say it; remember how I told you I used to come down here as a boy?

Yes.

Well the personal reason I came here was to see if I could track down my father. My biological father.

Will pauses, compelling Jasmine to ask:

And?

And I found him.

So who is he, Willy?

Will takes another moment and then answers slowly:

Clarence Hollister the 3rd.

Jasmine stares at Will, at first stunned, shaken, but then she begins to reconsider and smirks:

Nice try, Willy. Had me goin for a second there.

But Will's serious:

It's not a joke. I wish it was, but it's not.

Jasmine doesn't know how to react:

If you're...suggestin what I think you're suggestin—

I am.

Jasmine balks:

No way. Not possible.

That's what I thought, too. But not only is it possible, it's the way it is, whether I like it or not.

Jasmine's eyes fill with a growing agitation and anger:

Prove it.

Mona Rose Blessington.

Jasmine's face stiffens with recognition:

*Otherwise known as 'Megan', died giving birth to me,
Jasmine. At which point I was adopted by a family who moved
north. Which, I'm wagering, you probably still remember like it
was yesterday.*

Jasmine has to steady herself, rocked by the news. She then
stares at Will as a customer motions for Jasmine:

Could I get some coffee over here this week, please?

But Jasmine ignores him and marches right out of the diner
with Will now on her heels.

As she jumps into her Rambler, Will persists:

*Which makes me your half-brother, giving me a half-
interest claim in the Pinch.*

Now you're really tellin stories, Willy!

*Am I? Want me to take you to where our mother is buried?
Want me to take a DNA test? Cause I will.*

Get away from me and stay away from me!

Jasmine fires up the Rambler as Will informs her:

*And I for one am selling my half interest in the Pinch to my
father, Jasmine.*

Over my dead body, Willy!

Jasmine accelerates away, kicking up a cloud of dust as she
races away.

A half hour later, Hollister leans back in his office chair
with a wry, skeptical expression:

You actually expect me ta believe you're my long lost seed?

Will stares at him, grim:

*Imagine my thrill. But a DNA test will put the final nail in
that coffin. Meanwhile, I've got a proposition for you.*

Such as?

*I could use some cash, and I understand you could use an
interest in the Pinch.*

Hollister hadn't thought of that angle. And he's intrigued:

But what if it turns out ya aren't mine?

*Look, I'll sign anything you want me to, because if I'm not
who I say I am, between bringing me up on fraud charges, and
making sure I'm disbarred back home, I'm the one with the
downsides here. But if I am who I say I am, then you've got at
least half of what you want, and at better price than you'd*

*otherwise get it at a foreclosure auction, am I right? Especially
with all that oil out there.*

I'm listenin.

*So perhaps if we could both set aside all the warm and
fuzzy feelings of our long-delayed reunion, we could get down to
business?*

Meanwhile, Jasmine, ready with her own plan, is seated in
Dewey's office. He checks his watch and looks over at her:

Time, honey?

It's time, Jasmine.

As Will walks out of Hollister's office, he sees Jasmine on
her way in. She doesn't so much as look his way, so Will
continues on, in full possession of what he's doing.

A moment later, as Jasmine walks into Hollister's office, he
looks up, amazed to see her.

My. This day's just full of surprises.

I accept, Clarence.

Hollister can't resist playing dumb:

Accept what, Jasmine?

*You know damn well what, Clarence. But my price is this:
all the charges against Katie are ta be dropped. Forever. Deal?*

Hollister's face creams with a victory grin.

As Will sits in a swing in the park with the cannon,
Hollister arrives with a briefcase.

Will looks up:

Just like I said she would.

Hollister admits:

Just like ya said.

Hollister hands over the briefcase:

*Pleasure doin business with ya, Mr. Woods, or whoever
you are. And I won't be offended if ya'd care ta count it.*

No need, Mr. Mayor. You have a nice day now.

Back at the cottages, as the afternoon seems to simmer in
its oppressive heat, Jasmine and Katie drive back up in her
Rambler silently, sure that all is lost.

As they walk in to Jasmine's kitchen, they find the briefcase on the kitchen table with a note that states:

Hide this. Then tell Hollister the deal's off! - Will.

Jasmine reads the note, first in shock, then in anger, and then with eyes that suddenly register an entirely alternate possibility, Katie reads the note:

What does this mean? What this about?

…Willy.

Jasmine opens the briefcase to find fifteen hundred in cash.

As Jasmine's mind races to understand Will's gambit, Hollister, back in town at the restaurant, raises a victory toast with his cronies:

Did I or did I not say the Pinch would be ours, gentlemen? To the swamp, gentlemen, and to the wealth it hides from ordinary men.

They all toast, only too ready to admire themselves as Hollister winks:

And to the 'gators, who taught me everything I know!

Halfway through their steaks, they hear a commotion, and look up to see Jasmine forcing her way into their private luncheon. The restaurant's host tries to stop her:

Jasmine, ya can't just—

Just watch me, Earl!

Jasmine steps right up to Hollister's table, and Hollister looks up coolly, sure of his legal footing and victory:

Why Jasmine, to what do I owe the honor?

I've changed my mind, Clarence.

Excuse me?

You know how women-folk are: always changin our little minds. Anyway, deal's off. Just thought ya should know. But go on, boys, soak your troubles on me.

Jasmine throws down a hundred dollar bill, at which Hollister's eyes burn:

Katie's gonna regret your change of mind.

She's a woman. She'll understand.

She then nods to the room as she walks out:

Boys.

Hollister's cronies watch after her, confused, and then look to Hollister for an explanation, with deep concern on their faces:

A minor inconvenience, gentlemen. Nothin ta worry bout. She changed her mind once, and like she said, she'll change it again, especially by the time I get through with her.

As Jasmine strides back out onto the street, she sees Will, hanging out across the street, apparently waiting for her.

So she walks across the street and follows him around the side of a building, where they can talk safely, out of view.

When they're finally alone, she eases up to him and suddenly hauls off and slaps him!

As Will winces, taken off-guard, she slaps him again.

Then just when he thinks she's going to hit him again, she suddenly pounces and kisses him deeply.

After a long, lingering smooch, she pulls back and, eyes a beat and then slaps him yet again – only to dive back in for one more moving kiss. Finally:

Somebody's been tellin stories, Willy.

He shrugs, not sure if she's going to hit him again:

I hear tell it's kinda a tradition down here. But don't worry. You'll get used to it.

Her frustration and anger spent for the moment, she begins to tear up, and this time he kisses her, their emotions melting away into the sultry air.

As they drive back to their cottage park homes, Jasmine warns:

He's gonna be comin for ya, ya know that, don't ya?

I'm counting on that.

Jasmine looks over, more worried:

Sure? Hope you know how this story you're tellin turns out, Willy.

Will draws in a nervous breath:

The money safe?

Safest place I know.

A steady rain is falling as Jasmine and Will arrive back to see Sheriff Reynolds' cruiser.

As she pulls to a stop by her cottage, Reynolds climbs out and walks over to the Rambler's passenger side.

Mr. Woods, you're under arrest.

Will looks up dryly:

Why I'm shocked, flabbergasted and flummoxed.

Reynolds opens the Rambler's door, motioning Will out. Will obeys as Reynolds advises:

You could make it a lot easier on yourself by just tellin me where ya hid the Mayor's money.

Money? What money?

Reynolds shrugs as if he means 'have it your way' and handcuffs him.

Jasmine's eyes meanwhile dart around, worried to see Officer Hales searching the grounds.

But when he angles near Moo Moo's cottage, Moo Moo steps out with her trusty shotgun:

And just what do ya think you're doin?

Officer Hales slows, thinks better, and retreats to search elsewhere as Moo Moo trades a subtle, knowing glance with Jasmine.

If you were an impartial observer watching this moment play out, you might just conclude with a pretty darn good sense of certainty exactly where the money was hidden.

Later, as Reynolds drives Will back to the holding cells, he tries to warn Will:

Ya playin with fire. Ya know that, don't ya?

I'm not playing, Sheriff. Any more than you are.

They trade a look via the rear view mirror, and Will adds:

And that's why you're going to be interested in what I have to say.

Reynolds shrugs:

Unless it's about the Mayor's money, I ain't.

It's about Katie.

Reynolds pauses and eyes Will via the mirror again:

What about her?

Still later, as Will cools his heels in a holding cell, Hollister strolls in.

Whoever ya are, or whoever ya think ya are, I want my money back. Now.

Will looks up, confused:

What money?

Hollister's old, razor eyes sharpen:

That, my friend, was the wrong, damn answer.

Stepping next door, into Reynolds' office, Hollister oozes out his venom:

I want ya ta come down hard on this one, Sheriff. Real hard. Understand?

Reynolds leans back in his chair, as if perplexed:

I said: do ya understand?

Well, now, see, that's the thing, Mr. Mayor. Unless we can find that cash ya say he took under false pretenses, or we can prove criminal intent ta defraud, we gonna have one heck of a time—

You want proof? I'll show ya proof!

Hollister takes out the signed contract:

Here's your proof! In black and white. A signed contract.

He slaps it down on Reynolds' desk, just as Officer Hales enters the room, at which Reynolds turns to Hales:

Officer Hales, you'll be glad ta know the Mayor here has just handed me a document he says is a contract signed by the detainee Mr. Woods, proving he took the Mayor's money.

Reynolds looks back to Hollister:

Would that be a fair description, Mr. Mayor?

Yes, damn it. Now read it!

Reynolds picks up the contract for the first time and looks it over...

And you'd swear on a stack of Bibles that this here is the actual contract itself?

Absolutely!

Reynolds commences in the slow, gotcha southern way:

Then it looks like we got a problem.

Hollister grimaces:

What are ya talkin about?

Reynolds holds up the contract:

This here document has been signed by a William Hollister. Not a Will Woods.

Hollister grabs the contract back to see the signature and then quickly adjusts his claim:

Ain't no problem. Why, it only goes to show the extent of the fraud he's tried ta perpetrate.

Reynolds looks to Hales and then back at Hollister:

Is he your son, Mr. Mayor?

Course not!

So if ya knew he wasn't your son, who's defraudin who?

Hollister's eyes darken, and he turns to Hales:

Would you excuse us for a moment, Officer?

Officer Hales obliges and leaves the room.

The instant he exits, Hollister whips back around to confront Reynolds:

Just what the goddamn hell do ya think you're doin?

I'm gonna have ta release him, Mayor.

Hollister's face tightens with rage:

You let him go, and I'll make damn sure you get let go next, Sheriff.

But Reynolds just sits there, unmoved and unimpressed, enraging Hollister all the more:

Are ya really that big of a fool?

Reynolds doesn't respond, so Hollister marches into the holding cells to confront Will:

Think ya can play with me? Think ya can come down here like some carpetbagger and ride roughshod in my backyard?

I don't know what you're talking about.

Hollister's face fills with fire, but he carefully measures out his words:

If ya don't tell me where my money's, and I mean right now, you're gonna be sorry ya ever set foot in this here county. I can guarantee it.

What are you going to do, Mr. Mayor, take me out to the swamp, like you did Cassius and Mason?

Hollister steps in, close to the bars. They're face to face now:

I'm capable of just about anything ya can think of, and then some.

You would kill your own son over a pinch of land?

90

That Pinch of land, as ya call it, is worth more than any blood, Mr. Woods. Ta say nothing of carpetbaggers.

Besides, just between you, me and the moon, from the very moment that woman's womb corrupted my seed, and turned it inta that abomination of a man, all he ever was ta me was a humiliatin vexation. A curse. Not ta mention an ingrate who thought he could turn his back on his responsibilities and commitments. Well he can't turn his back on me now, can he? So, yes, son, I put him outta his misery with my own hand, just like I can put you oughta yours.

Will shrugs:

You already have, actually. In fact you've put us all out of our misery.

Hollister's eyes cinch:

What are you talkin about, boy?

The miracle of digital recording.

Will points up at a video camera monitoring the room.

Hollister peers up at it, momentarily concerned, but then looks back to Will with a sneer:

Sorry, but that camera's deaf as mud. Oh it can see is us talking, but it can't hear a word of what we're sayin, son. So unless ya got—

Will pulls out his cellphone:

One of these?

Hollister's face cinches but then eases:

A phone, Mr. Woods? Best use that ta call yourself a lawyer.

Actually, I am a lawyer, Mr. Mayor. And while this is indeed a phone, it also has this little record function built right in, and, as you can see, it's recording.

Will points out the little meter reacting to their voices, and Hollister turns pale:

Amazing, huh? Anyway, you combine this recording with that camera, and the rest, as they say, is up to a jury of your peers.

Hollister sobers, his mind racing, scrambling for a way out as Sheriff Reynolds steps calmly into the cell block, just as Hollister, thinking he's found that way out, offers Will a strange grin:

Very well, Mr. Woods. You win.

Hollister looks to Reynolds:

In fact, I respect a man who goes after what he wants and don't let anythin get in his way. Ain't that right, Sheriff? So the only question now is: what is it that ya want?

Reynolds suddenly realizes the Mayor means him.

What I want? I want the peace of mind that comes from knowin justice has been served.

At which Reynolds opens a jail cell for Hollister, and holds it open for him.

So Hollister plays his last card:

Ah come on now, Sheriff, you know I was bluffin him about Cassius, don't ya? Surely ya know that. I was bluffin ta scare that Mr. Woods inta telling the truth. Hell, a little misdirection is basic ta any interrogation. You of all people should know that.

Reynolds holds the cell door open for Hollister.

And what if I refuse, Sheriff?

I don't see addin a charge of resistin arrest is gonna help ya case any, Mayor.

Hollister, seething, finally enters the cell:

I wonder if ya'd mind contactin my lawyer for me, Sheriff. And ya might wanna contact yours as well.

If ya had one, I would. But don't worry, I'll get yours on the horn right away.

The streets glisten, wet from the downpour as Will and Reynolds step out into the clear night to see Jasmine waiting across the street for them.

She comes over, indicating she wants to go in to see Hollister:

Mind if I have a word with the prisoner?

Reynolds nods:

Suit yourself.

Will moves to join her, but Jasmine waves him off – she wants this moment with Clarence all to herself.

A minute later, Jasmine walks in to find Hollister behind bars, defiant as ever.

Never looked better, Clarence. Jail suits ya.

They think they got me, but they ain't got me, any more than you got me, Jasmine.

Ya got yourself, Clarence.

Contrary ta what ya may think, I didn't kill Cassius. Fact, I always figured it was you, Jasmine.

Wasn't me, Clarence. So if ya don't mind, I'll go right on believin it was you.

Careful, little girl. Your hate's gonna make ya even blinder than your love. But either way, I'm gonna get out from under this, and when I do, believe me, you'll rue the day ya ever crossed me.

Jasmine eyes him a moment – a world of wounds, rage and revenge lifting, releasing like the mists off the swamp:

Don't ever change, honey; I wanna forget ya just the way you are.

Jasmine nods, turns and walks out, leaving Hollister to his own little hell.

As Will and Reynolds wait for her outside, Reynolds looks at Will:

So what did ya do with all that money?

Will considers it and then answers honestly:

It belongs to Jasmine.

Will waits to see how he'll react as Reynolds absorbs it; he then nods to Will, satisfied with that outcome.

So just between you, me and the moon, who did kill Cassius and Mason?

Reynolds looks at Will a long, opaque beat before answering:

Wasn't the Mayor.

As Will's face flushes with surprise:

But no matter, Clarence done enough in his day ta deserve everythin he's got comin ta him.

So...who was it?

Reynolds draws in a slow breath as they stand there in the dark and then he says:

Mason beat Katie up one too many times, Mr. Woods. Just like Cassius done Jasmine. A man can't stand for that sort of thing. Not in my town.

Their eyes lock, and Will realizes it was Reynolds all along, and by constantly going after Jasmine and Katie, he was keeping them close, safe from Hollister.

Sensing that Will now has his answer, Reynolds nods:

I trust ya won't go writin anythin that might hurt Jasmine and Katie anymore than they already been hurt.

You have my word.

Reynolds accepts that as Will's bond.

Ya have yourself a pleasant evenin, Mr. Woods.

Will watches after Reynolds lumbers back into his office, nodding to Jasmine as she comes out to see the look on Will's thunderstruck face:

Ya all right?

As he continues to stare after Reynolds, he ekes out a small, revelatory nod.

Days later, Jasmine drives Will up to a mail box. Will gets out with a packet of divorce documents and moves to the post box, scribbling out a note:

'Redo. Brenda deserves better. Make it fair. - Will.'

He seals the note in the envelope, drops the packet into the mail box, and then climbs back into the Rambler.

That evening, down on the Pinch, Will and Jasmine lean back against a tree, taking in the orange and lavender streaked sky of the evening.

There's just one thing I don't get: why couldn't ya just tell me?

If it was going to work, I needed both of you to believe my story. At least until he bit the bait. What I didn't expect was Reynolds' help.

Neither did I. Bu then maybe Clarence was right about one thing: my hate blinded me worse than love. Anyway, thank heavens for Dewey, too.

How so?

The Pinch is a nature preserve.

Will looks over at Jasmine, confused, when she adds:

I donated the Pinch. To the Nature Conservancy. Dewey arranged everythin. This here's gonna be a wild life refuge.

As he takes an amazed moment to wrap his head around it, Jasmine continues:

Hollister and his kind weren't never gonna get it, honey. Trust me.

So you were holding out on me?

That makes two of us, darling. ...So ya think you'll ever find your biological father?

No. But I found something else.

Will gives Jasmine a knowing look: he's referring to her. A subtle but dire wave of relief washes over Jasmine.

That mean you're stayin?

That depends on whether you plan on disappearing. You know, like some women do.

Not if you don't vanish on me, I won't.

So: no more alibis?

Her eyes mist:

Well, Willy, looks like we got each other by the hind legs, huh?

Will has to grin:

That would be nice.

As Jasmine cracks up, she tucks herself under his arm:

My, my, Willy, you do go on.

Yes we do.

She smiles, and gazes out at the swamp's lush and wild expanse.

...Yes we do.

Just then, a loon called out in the warm, humid air as a bullfrog croaked in the swamp grasses and an alligator floated slyly away, submerging once more into the blue-dappled waters to doze.

But when evening fell, and Will and Jasmine had returned to her cottage, one bachelor cricket could finally put away his incessant night songs and longings, set aside his long-held misapprehensions and deeply buried wounds, let go of his rationales and defenses and alibis and rest in the life-changing surprise that is love – a love that had found and recognized him in the darkness, long before he had ever recognized himself.

~*~

Raised in Los Angeles, Darryl Sollerh's recent works include
"SHaDOW GAME", a Reader Views FIRST PLACE AWARD
winner, as well as "MINDFALL", "TRANCER", "EDDY
FALLS" and "COWBOY AND INDIAN", a Readers' Favorite
SILVER MEDAL AWARD winner. All are now available in
print, as well as on Kindle, iPad, Nook and eReaders everywhere.
For more, visit www.DarrylSollerh.com

~*~

For Savannah

~*~

www.ingramcontent.com/pod-product-compliance
Lightning Source LLC
Chambersburg PA
CBHW020628130626
46552CB00003B/1129